BY THE SAME AUTHOR

Fiction

Fightback

STILL FIGHTING

To Leo
with Best Wishes
Russ

Still Fighting

Published by The Conrad Press Ltd. in the United Kingdom 2023

Tel: +44(0)1227 472 874
www.theconradpress.com
info@theconradpress.com

ISBN 978-1-915494-39-9

Printed and bound in Great Britain by Clays Ltd, Elcograf S.p.A

Typesetting and cover design by The Book Typesetters
www.thebooktypesetters.com

The Conrad Press logo was designed by Maria Priestley.

STILL FIGHTING

Thomas Chapman

For Irene

Who has constantly encouraged me to write

1.

ennis McMillan packed away the rifle, telescopic sight and silencer and swiftly made his way from his covert hideaway next to the canal bank. He carefully removed any trace of having been camped in the trees by the side of the towpath canal. He packed away discarded plastic sandwich wrappings and empty polystyrene cups which had once contained nourishment to sustain him during his vigil. With his boot he raked up the earth in an attempt to return the patch of ground back to normality. He had a quick last look at his hide and left the scene.

He walked quickly across the large expanse of fields known as Hackney Marshes back towards the car park next to the sport's grounds changing rooms. Once back inside his motor vehicle he took out his mobile phone and texted to a number listed in his phone records:

Job done. Update me on reports

Almost instantly he received a reply:

Well done, your request noted.

McMillan had just shot Albert Oxford. He had just committed a murder. Oxford had been directly, or indirectly involved in the deaths of at least six people including that of McMillan's friend, Detective Superintendent William Cronk. McMillan gave thought to what he had just done. Well, who would miss Albert Oxford? The world certainly wouldn't miss him.

His friend Cronk had been in charge of an investigation into the murder of two young black people in Tottenham. One of the victims was a young innocent waitress called Marcia Williams and the other was Joshua Mills who had belonged to a north London crime gang which operated under the name of Black Lightning This enquiry was linked to a series of killings in east London orchestrated by Albert Oxford and various accomplices.

The East London killings investigation was compromised by the involvement of two Metropolitan Police detectives who were manipulating Oxford and his associates. The two detectives had been killed in an incident at Holborn Underground station. The corrupt procedures and subsequent deaths of these two policemen had resulted in Oxford avoiding prosecution.

Oxford had retired to Spain to enjoy the warmer climes and relaxed lifestyle which he couldn't enjoy in East London. McMillan smiled to himself thinking that Oxford's plan had not worked out as planned. Good riddance, thought McMillan.

McMillan himself had been a Metropolitan Police Officer before leaving the Force prematurely after he had unlawfully discharged a firearm whilst working for the Specialist Firearms Unit of the Metropolitan Police. He had loved being a police officer and was fully intending to serve out his time in the Force. The unfortunate incident which foreshortened his career and ruined his reputation could have been avoided but his impetuosity had got the better of him and an innocent member of the public suffered a serious firearms wound from which he eventually recovered. McMillan's police career, though, was finished.

He had made friends with Cronk during their rugby-playing days and this friendship had been forged after McMillan left the Force. McMillan had moved to Spain and worked as a private investigator. Cronk had visited him on several occasions and the pair enjoyed eating and drinking together and reminiscing about the good old days.

When Cronk had sought his help he had no hesitation in putting himself at Cronk's disposal. Cronk had told McMillan that he was terminally ill and wanted to right some wrongs that had occurred in the last few months of Cronk's police service. He wanted to confront Albert Oxford who was now resident in Spain.

It had been easy for McMillan, using his private investigator's skills, to track down Oxford. McMillan had met Cronk at the airport and later had supplied him with a firearm to carry out the deed.

The meeting between Cronk and Oxford had not worked out as planned. Cronk indeed did shoot Oxford, but not fatally. He sustained a head wound to his left temple. Cronk, believing that he had killed Oxford, and with no prospect of any meaningful life in the future because of his terminal illness, had turned the gun on himself and died immediately.

Oxford was hospitalised and spent some time in a Spanish hospital. After an investigation into the shootings by the Spanish Guardia, a decision was made by the Spanish authorities to ask Albert Oxford to leave Spain.

McMillan now found himself back in the United Kingdom attempting to finish off the job that his old friend, William Cronk, had wanted carried out.

McMillan sat in his vehicle in the car park next to the changing rooms and decided he was not going to spend any more time in the UK but that he would return to Spain to continue his business of private investigations and other enterprises.

Twenty-four hours later McMillan would be back in Spain.

2.

On the towpath of the River Lea Navigation Canal, a middle-aged couple walking their dog heard the sound of another dog barking frantically. Sensing that the other dog was in distress, they made their way towards the sound and saw that the dog, a brown and white Jack Russell, was standing on the bow of a canal boat and was barking furiously at something in the water.

Leaving his own dog with his wife some yards away, the man peered into the water and saw the body of a man floating, face down in the stagnant water.

Without hesitation the man jumped fully clothed into the water. Fortunately the water was only about five feet deep. He grabbed hold of the man's jacket and attempted to turn him face-upwards. He yelled at his wife to call the Emergency Services.

After he had turned the man over, he attempted to get him next to the bank but this proved to be difficult as the bottom of the canal varied in depth and the underfoot conditions were slippery.

Slowly he inched himself and the man towards the side of the canal. By now the inhabitants of a neighbouring canal boat on hearing the commotion and prolonged barking had come forward to help both men out of the water.

The rescuer was able to assist himself whilst the man who had been floating had to be dragged from the water. He looked in a bad way and the situation was not helped by the brown and white Jack Russell constantly licking his face.

The rescued man was placed in the recovery position and within a very short space of time a motor bike paramedic was on scene and took charge of the situation.

He thought he could detect a pulse but it was very weak. He cleared the patient's airways and after covering the man with a foil blanket, waited for the ambulance to get as close as it could to the scene of the incident.

BBC London News

Police are investigating the shooting of a man on a canal boat moored on the River Lea Navigation Canal. The unnamed man was taken by ambulance to Homerton Hospital. Police are appealing for witnesses...

Two doctors and a nursing sister stood by the bed of the man who had been brought in from the River Lea Navigation Canal. The man was attached to a variety of machines which blinked numbers and made beeping noises.

'I don't know how this man is alive. He must have the

constitution of an ox.'

'Yes, he's not only survived being shot but survived drowning as well. And from what I've heard being licked to death and given artificial resuscitation by a puppy,' smiled the other doctor.

'Indeed. It's a shame we don't have this man's medical records, but there's no doubt that the metal plate inserted in his left temple saved his life.'

3.

ennis McMillan's plane landed in shimmering heat and taxied to arrivals. Once he had cleared Customs he made his way to the long-term car park and drove his car south along the motorway towards the little village where he lived.

His villa was a large, sprawling three-bedroomed house with gardens, a swimming pool and an attached garage that served as an office where he had set up his computer and other equipment that he used when working as a licensed private investigator.

The ample garage space also contained enough room for his motor vehicle, a big comfortable SEAT Leon estate, but this was almost usually parked to the side of the driveway under a canvas awning to protect it from the glare of the sun.

McMillan entered his kitchen area through the rear of the house. His wife Rosa was bent over a hotplate preparing a Spanish stew.

McMillan grunted a greeting at her and she responded in similar fashion. The early passion of their romance some ten years ago had long since faded but they suffered each other's company.

In McMillan's case he treated Rosa as a glorified house-keeper who tended to the house, gardens and swimming pool. She provided meals when McMillan was at home.

Rosa suffered life with Dennis McMillan. Although he was surly and non-communicative, he had never been violent or abusive to her. She had a circle of friends, all women with one notable exception, who she would regularly lunch with.

Rosa and her young beau, Alberto, had met at one of Rosa's lunch-time soirees and had had the odd passionate liaison. Alberto had been pleading with Rosa to leave McMillan but her existence at her marital home had not been that desperate. She enjoyed her home comforts.

McMillan's long-term plan was to make enough money to enable him to split with Rosa and to move on to pastures new, notably in the shapely form of his girlfriend, Carmela.

McMillan's wife Rosa intended to hang on as long as she could. She knew that McMillan would not be here forever. It would eventually free her to carry on with a near to normal lifestyle which would obviously involve Alberto.

The only problem with McMillan's partner, Carmela, was her father, Carlos. He was known locally as El Caballo - the horse. He was a small-time gangster who possessed a fearsome reputation. He ruled his own little community with a fist of iron and was feared by most, if not all of the inhabitants.

There was no love lost between McMillan and El Caballo as McMillan had acted as the private investigator when helping Caballo's wife in obtaining a divorce from the Horse.

After partaking of some of Rosa's stew, McMillan retired to the garage which acted as his office. McMillan checked the machinery and his burner mobile phone but he didn't see or hear the message he was hoping for. There was no news of the death of Albert Oxford.

He pinged off a message to his contact in London:

Any news?

He waited for a reply and checked his other messages and emails. Routine, run-of-the-mill stuff that could be handled comfortably. He would give most of these to Mateo, his assistant.

There was one message however, that caught his eye. He recognised the sender's pseudonym:

Delivery due.

McMillan replied with a thumbs-up emoji.

McMillan's mobile beeped with another message which he read:

Nothing yet, the project may have failed. I'll give it a few days and investigate.

McMillan frowned and replied:

Keep me updated.

4.

I t took Albert Oxford a few days to regain full consciousness. When he came to, he looked at his surroundings. He was wired to a couple of machines which flashed numbers constantly. Canulars had been fitted to both arms and he was aware that he had been hooked up to a catheter.

He appeared to be in a private room in a hospital as there were no other beds containing patients. Sitting by the door was a uniformed police officer reading a book.

A young doctor, accompanied by an even younger student and a stoutly built nurse entered Albert's room.

'Welcome back to the land of the living,' said the young doctor with a smile. 'You've had an extremely lucky escape. Someone took a potshot at you but the bullet hit a metal plate which had been inserted in your head.'

'I received that little present in a Spanish hospital. Thank goodness for the Spanish medicos.'

'Yes indeed,' said the doctor. 'You will obviously be with us for a few days but because it would appear that someone has taken a dislike to you, the police will maintain a presence here in this part of the building.'

'Mr Oxford, the police will want to interview you

formally. Detective Sergeant Fuller from Hackney Police station will probably be here tomorrow. You don't have to speak to him if it will upset you.'

'No, it's okay. I'm happy to speak with the sergeant. I've got nothing to hide,' said Albert

The following morning, Albert was washed and cleaned by two nurses. He had his bed sheets changed. He was propped up on two comfortable pillows. He was told, on asking, that he was currently a resident in Homerton Hospital.

After breakfast and a mid-morning mug of tea, Albert was visited by Detective Sergeant Fuller from Hackney Police station. Fuller was a dapper man who wore a light coloured raincoat and a brown trilby hat which he removed and held when entering Albert's room. Fuller reminded Albert of an old film star with his pencil-thin clipped moustache. Fuller introduced himself.

'Mr Oxford, it would appear that someone's got it in for you. Your details flag up all over the place. You get a serious mention in the case of the killings in East London last year but because of complications involving two Metropolitan Police officers you've avoided prosecution. I've just learned that you were involved at the scene of the death of a former Detective Chief Inspector, William Cronk, who died in a Spanish seaside town. He took his own life after attempting to kill you.'

'You were hospitalised and during that stay you had a metal plate inserted in your head, something that has saved your life on this latest occasion. After a less than satisfactory investigation by the Spanish Guardia, the authorities in

Spain decided that they didn't want your presence gracing Spanish soil.'

'Am I doing okay so far Mr Oxford?' asked Detective Sergeant Fuller.

'Not bad,' replied Albert. 'But who shot me and more importantly, what happened to my dog?'

'Your dog's being taken care of by one of your canal boat neighbours. As for the shooter we haven't got a lot to go on. We've seized the CCTV footage from the Sports Ground car park and we're currently trawling through that. But otherwise, I was hoping you might be able to help me.'

'Sorry,' Albert replied. 'If I think of anything you'll be the first to know.'

DS Fuller ignored the sarcasm and said,

'I might be stating the obvious, Mr Oxford, but I'll repeat what I said earlier that someone has obviously got it in for you. I would impress upon you that you shouldn't return to your canal boat. If you'll forgive my attempt at humour, you'll be a sitting duck on the canal.'

Albert smiled.

'Thank you, sergeant, I'll heed your advice.'

5.

As Albert lay in his hospital bed he had plenty of time to contemplate the advice of the detective and in particular to avoid returning to his canal boat. His concern for Bart, his Jack Russell puppy, had dissipated on learning that he was being cared for. It was probably Kevin and Caroline that lived three boats upstream from his boat.

Albert pondered his immediate problem. In the past he had found friendships easy to foster. His neighbours in East London had been solid people. His next-door neighbour Harry had been one of his staunchest allies in the fightback against the criminal element in his neighbourhood. But, it now appeared that Harry was not in very good health and had moved with his wife, to be nearer his sister-in-law out in the sticks at Southend in Essex.

Another of his accomplices was a huge Pole, Lech, who had returned to his native country with his wife Annelka. They had been forced away by the situation in their neighbourhood and had returned to Poland with the intention of fostering or adopting children.

Their plan however, had been thwarted by the Polish Authorities discovering Lech's alleged involvement in various suspicious deaths in the Stratford area of east London.

Last, but not least, Albert thought fondly of his friend Eddie Baines who had been landlord and genial host of the Princess Victoria public house. The pub had been at the epicentre of the fightback, but poor old Eddie had sadly succumbed to the virus which had swept the world. Albert still got upset that he had never had the chance to say his good-byes to his great friend.

After the incident in Spain involving William Cronk, Albert had lived a quiet contented existence on his canal boat. His new found friend Bart the puppy had entertained and amused him. He enjoyed a glass of wine whilst listening to his classical music tapes or tuning in to Classic FM on his radio.

Albert, of course, needed human interaction. It wasn't enough to speak to Bart as he did almost continuously. The dog had dutifully pretended that he understood everything his master said by cocking his head to the side.

So it was that Albert had made use of a public house he had discovered in the back-doubles of Hackney. The pub was called the Plume of Feathers. It was only a fifteen minute walk from the canal boat and although not the nearest pub, it contained an interesting mix of characters.

The licensee was a very large lady of ample proportions who was permanently ensconced on the bar stool at one end of the long wooden oak bar. A pair of metal-framed glasses was perched on the end of her nose through which she kept a beady eye on the clientele and the two tills.

Margaret was not averse to over-running the prescribed

licensing hours and these 'shut-outs' as they were known by the customers, fuelled a happy atmosphere of bonhomie within the bars of the public house.

Albert's favourite part of the pub was the bar known as the 'snug' bar. It was not a big bar and was dominated by three tables which seemed to be permanently occupied by customers playing dominoes. There was a fierce, but friendly edge to the competitions. Albert enjoyed this competitiveness and joined in on occasions.

The centre-piece and star of this group was a real interesting character. Father Michael Creaney was a Catholic priest who carried out his religious duties at the church of St Paul which was situated between Hackney and Stoke Newington.

Father Michael was a popular figure. He was partial to a glass of Guinness and on many occasions had been spotted stumbling hap-hazardly back to his living quarters adjoining the chapel situated near Stoke Newington Green.

He was also one of the star exponents of the game of dominoes. He possessed a bright cheery countenance with a florid face to match, and which contained an almost permanent smile. Father Michael had taken to Albert and had welcomed him to the flock although Albert had pointed out that he was not a man of religion.

'There's plenty of time for you yet,' the Father had told him in a soft Irish brogue.

Another of the regulars who Albert had taken to was an elderly gentleman of West Indian extraction called Nobby. Nobby had retired from a lifetime of work with London Transport. Nobby was also an expert at the game of dominoes.

'He can knock back the Guiness, can Father Michael,'

Albert had said to Nobby as they sat watching a game whilst cuddling their own pints of ale.

'He sure can. He took me once to the horse racing at Cheltenham one year because he knew I liked a bet,' replied Nobby.

'When we arrived at the races early he took me straight to the Guinness tent. You couldn't believe it Albert, but there must have been about 2,000 pre-poured pints of the black stuff just waiting to be topped up. He started drinking the stuff at half past ten in the morning.'

'You're not going to tell me he drank the lot?' said Albert, smiling.

'No,' replied Nobby, smiling, 'but I left him to it and went out to enjoy the racing. You couldn't believe the amount of Irish priests gambling and drinking,' said Nobby. 'After the last race he was still in the Guinness tent but was the worse for wear. I managed to pour him back onto the train home. He never saw a horse all day.'

Albert had warmed to another member of the group, Peter who worked in Westminster and worked at junior level within the Home Office.

'He's very touchy about his hair. Best not to mention it,' Peter had told him.

'What do you mean?' asked Albert.

'You must have noticed Albert. The hair on top of his head is not his but has been borrowed from some animal.'

Albert hadn't noticed but on the next domino group meeting he became fixated by looking at the attachment to the Father's head. Sure enough, the grey wispy bits did not match the luxuriant, shiny, groomed mop sitting atop his head. Father Michael caught Albert staring at it but Albert quickly looked away.

Whilst Albert was contemplating the advice given to him by DS Fuller, a nurse popped her head round the door of his private room.

'You have a visitor Mr Oxford. The police officer on sentry duty here has given permission for this man to visit you and he's been cleared. He said his name is Nobby and that you would know who he was.'

Albert was pleased to see Nobby.

'How did you know I was here Nobby?' asked Albert.

'There was a report on television, Albert, and it said that the shooting had occurred near the canal. Knowing that you lived on a canal boat and the fact that we've missed you at the Plume made me think it could be you. Nearest hospital to the canal and here I am.'

'Well done Sherlock. I'm pleased to see you.'

Once the small-talk had finished, Albert said to Nobby,

'I've a problem that I need to overcome Nobby, insomuch as I'm now homeless. I can't go back to the boat for a while as somebody is trying to kill me. It means that I have to keep my head down and keep a low profile. I'm struggling to think of somewhere.'

'Albert, have you considered asking Father Michael? Over the years he has had a record of looking after waifs and strays and it looks like you'd qualify in that category now.'

Albert lay back on his pillow and considered what Nobby had just said. It made sense but, of course, he would have to speak to the Father.

6.

The following day Albert was having a snooze just after the hospital lunch. The nurse woke him and said,

'Another visitor, Mr Oxford and this one didn't have to be vetted.'

Standing behind her was the figure of Father Michael Creaney wearing his dog-collar and the garb of his religious vocation. His bright eyes twinkled and a smile creased his face.

'It's wonderful to see you alive and well Albert. We're already starting to miss you at the Plume. The sales of IPA beer are plummeting rapidly,' Father Michael said.

Albert thanked Michael for his kind words. The Father sat next to Albert's bed. He was wearing a crumpled dark blue suit with a black shirt and religious collar.

'Now, what are we doing here?' asked the priest.

'It's a long story Michael. Probably too long to relate now but when I get the chance to buy you a pint of Guinness I might tell you the whole story. But it's not a pretty picture and somebody has got it in for me.'

'It's true then that someone tried to kill you by shooting at you?' asked Michael.

'Yes, and if it hadn't been for this beautiful piece of Spanish metal' said Albert touching his left temple, 'I'd be a goner. But that's another story as well.'

'So my boy what are you going to do? You obviously can't go back to your canal boat.'

There was a prolonged silence. Albert looked at the priest.

'Then you'll come to live with me when you are ready to leave here, I've plenty of room at the chapel and the chapel house.'

Albert grabbed the Father's hand and squeezed it.

'Thank you' said Albert, 'that's so kind of you although I think I'll be here as a guest of the National Health Service for quite a while yet.'

'You can come and sort out the conditions of your residency with me when you are fit to leave. In the meantime I must attend to the demands of my flock,' said the priest.

'At the Plume of Feathers? asked Albert,

'I couldn't possibly comment, Albert,' said the priest with a wink.

7.

At Hackney Police station Detective Sergeant Fuller spent the afternoon trawling through the CCTV footage of the car park at the changing rooms at Hackney Marshes.

After innumerable cups of coffee, broken up by smoking-breaks in the designated smoking areas in the backyard of the station his attention was suddenly drawn to the evening that Albert Oxford had been shot, and in particular to a grainy piece of footage which showed an image approaching the car park from the direction of the football pitches. He appeared to be carrying a holdall. The man sat in a motor vehicle for about ten minutes before driving off.

Due to the darkness and quality of the camera, the vehicle's number plate could not be clearly identified but as the car reached the exit barrier the number plate was enhanced by the floodlight of a security camera. Fuller froze the image and uploaded the image onto an app.

Edward Fuller then rang a friendly contact at the Metropolitan Police Forensic Laboratory who promised Fuller that he would look at the image he was about to receive by email and he told Fuller he would ring him if and when he had a result with the number plate of the car.

Later that day Fuller looked at the message on his phone in astonishment. The message had come from his acquaintance at the Metropolitan Police Forensic Laboratory.

The vehicle had been identified by its number plate which had been captured on CCTV when leaving the Hackney Marshes car park. What was astonishing however, was that the registered owner of the vehicle was shown as William Cronk, the detective who had tried to murder Albert Oxford and had then taken his own life on that fateful sunny afternoon in a sleepy Spanish seaside town.

When Fuller went to Homerton Hospital, he saw that Albert Oxford was walking very tentatively round his room taking the first faltering steps towards recovery.

'Looks like it won't be long before you're out of here,' said Fuller

'A couple of days,' replied Albert.

'Before you leave Mr Oxford, you will need to furnish me with details of where you will be living. I appreciate it won't be the canal boat.'

'I'm just finalising arrangements,' replied Albert. 'Have you made any progress on my case?'

'There's been a development,' replied the detective, 'and one that is quite disturbing.'

'You've got my full attention Sergeant Fuller, this sounds quite exciting.'

'I've been trawling through CCTV footage from the night you were shot, and in particular the car park of the changing rooms at Hackney Marshes. My attention was drawn to a male person getting into a vehicle in the car park. The footage wasn't clear but once the images had been enhanced I was able to identify the registered owner of the vehicle.'

Fuller paused for dramatic effect.

'And?' Albert asked impatiently.

'The registered owner is a certain William Cronk.'

Albert looked dumbfounded.

'Sergeant, I'm not a gambling man, but I would be prepared to wager that it wasn't Cronk who shot me on this occasion. The last time I saw Cronk he looked decidedly unwell.'

'How astute of you,' replied Fuller, 'you would've made a great detective. A real loss to the Metropolitan Police Criminal Investigation Department.'

Ignoring Fuller's sarcasm Albert asked,

'What happens now then?'

'Details of the vehicle have been circulated and any sightings will be reported to me.'

8.

ennis McMillan had looked at his burner mobile which had said:

Delivery due

McMillan rang his trusted aide Mateo to tell him that they had to make another collection and arranged to meet him at the jetty where McMillan's small motor boat was moored.

Later that day and just after darkness had descended, McMillan started up the engine of the outboard motor and with Mateo aboard, slowly steered the boat out of the harbour and started their journey in a southerly direction. A light gentle breeze and calm waters made the journey bearable.

McMillan had enough fuel aboard for the journey he was undertaking and although an accomplished sailor he stuck to the shoreline where the twinkling lights ashore indicated business was getting back to near-normal after the pandemic.

McMillan checked an app on his phone and steered the craft towards a signal he was receiving from a tracking device.

The journey took almost two hours and necessitated leaving the shoreline for the last few kilometres.

As McMillan neared the tracking device signal he spotted a light attached to a buoy. A tracking device was attached to the buoy and this had guided McMillan to the target.

McMillan cut the engine and Mateo, in a well rehearsed manner, pulled the attached chain upwards. There was a consignment attached to the floating buoy. This was a four foot by three foot package wrapped with waterproof packaging.

After Mateo had removed the package with a degree of difficulty, McMillan assisted Mateo to secure the package at the back of the boat.

McMillan obviously knew what the package contained. He was not concerned with payment for the package as that was taken care of by his paymasters and involved a transfer of money by Hawala, an Indian money laundering operation.

McMillan mused that the collection of parcels from the depths of the sea must mean an increase in the value of the commodity as they were now using Hawala, the Indian money laundering process, instead of the usual crooked process previously used with Western Union.

McMillan restarted the engine and the boat, with its contents, retraced its route back towards the jetty it had left some four hours previously.

On return to the horseshoe-shaped jetty, Mcmillan coasted to the opposite side to where his craft was normally moored. Whilst he steadied the boat, Mateo skipped ashore and the two men between them hauled the package onto the stone pavings of the harbour. Mateo was able to manhandle the package into the back of a van which he used to transport fish from the harbour to the fish market.

Once McMillan had seen Mateo drive off with his cargo he returned his boat to its rightful mooring in the harbour.

9.

Dennis McMillan was pottering about in his garage-cum-office. His wife Rosa was preparing herself before going out to lunch with her circle of girlfriends, after which she would hook up with her young toy-boy Alberto. She knew that her husband was going out on his boat later that day so she wouldn't have to worry about catering for him.

Worried frowns creased McMillan's brow. He hadn't received confirmation from the news channels or his source in London that Oxford was dead. His failure to eliminate Albert Oxford meant he would have to take care of that eventually.

He also had to make another trip out to the buoy to satisfy the demands of criminal paymasters and his financial situation.

But before he made his trip he had another assignation to look forward to. He was taking his girlfriend Carmela out for some tapas and a glass of wine. McMillan had to be careful about being seen with Carmela as he knew first hand that her father, Carlos, known as El Caballo, was a violent thug.

McMillan and Carmela sat at a table away from the

entrance and windows. He had deliberately chosen a restaurant a few miles down the coast to keep them both away from prying eyes.

After partaking of some tapas dishes they prepared to leave to make the journey to a small Spanish hotel which they had used previously on numerous occasions.

McMillan asked for the bill from the waitress unaware that the cashier was staring at McMillan. He had recognised Carmela. He had noticed her before when she had attended a restaurant he used to work at. She had been having lunch with her father.

The cashier knew who her father was and, more importantly, his reputation. There was no mistaking Carmela as she was strikingly beautiful and he pondered why she was with this older man. He was squat, powerfully built and had an oversized head parked onto muscular shoulders and arms. His dark eyes were constantly on the lookout.

As McMillan and Carmela left the restaurant the cashier slipped out the rear door of the restaurant and carefully noted the number plate of the vehicle that McMillan was driving.

10.

N obby saw that Albert was ready to leave the hospital. He was dressed in the clothes that he had been wearing when he had been brought into hospital. The clothes mercifully had been washed and pressed by the nursing staff.

'Father Michael's expecting you Albert. I will drop you off at the chapel.'

Albert had never been inside a church, never mind the Catholic church of St Paul. He knew of the church and had walked past it on the odd occasion.

It was an imposing structure set in its own grounds. It lay back off the road opposite a large expanse of green.

Nobby drove his van up the driveway and saw that Father Creaney was standing at the entrance steps to the church, smiling from ear to ear as if he was greeting Sunday's congregation. He was wearing the robes of his office.

After Albert had been deposited, Nobby drove off, saying that he would catch up with Albert later at the Plume of Feathers. Albert shouted out a thank you and turned back to face Michael Creaney.

'Welcome to God's house Albert. Let me show you

around the premises.'

'Father, I have to repeat that I'm not a man of religion and I feel somewhat of a fraud.'

'Albert please don't worry about that. There will have been worse sinners than you under this roof.'

Albert muttered under his breath, 'I wouldn't bet on it.'

Father Michael led the way and proceeded to give Albert a tour of the premises. He led Albert through the impressive archway that formed the entrance of the church. The two large oak doors were fastened back to the front-facing wall and inside these doors there was a small vestibule area which contained a trestle table on which were several lit candles.

'These candles are lit by members of my congregation in memory of loved ones that have moved on,' said the Father. Albert wondered if he had been responsible for any of the candles that had been lit!

Albert and the priest then moved into the main body of the church. To Albert's unreligious eye, the view was dramatic. The first impression was the height of the church with its beautiful ornate ceiling. This roof appeared to be supported by a series of gilded columns placed down each side of the main bank of pews. Both walls had a series of stained glass windows.

On the other side of the columns were more narrower rows of pews lit by candles contained in tall holders. At the far end of the church behind the altar and table was a tall magnificent stained glass window depicting a religious scene of the Virgin Mary and a baby Jesus. The altar and pulpit were plainly stated and a candle holder with lit candles provided subdued lighting at this end of the church.

'What do you think Albert? asked the Father.

'Very impressive,' replied Albert.

On their way back down the aisle Michael pointed to a wooden structure on the side of the pews.

'That's the confessional box Albert. Maybe one day I'll get you in there and you can confess your sins to God.'

'It would take a couple of weeks,' replied Albert, 'but maybe one day. Don't build your hopes up yet though.'

The priest smiled and led Albert back outside into bright sunshine.

Separated from the church by a narrow alleyway was a two-storey brick building with its own front entrance.

'This is my private living quarters Albert, and if we go around the side of this building we can gain access to your new living quarters.'

Father Creaney led the way, after unlocking the heavy door. Once inside Albert was confronted with a set of concrete steps leading up to the living quarters.

At first-floor level Albert saw a passageway with three doors. Father Michael stopped outside the furthest door and said to Albert,

'Welcome to your new living quarters.' He opened the door with a key which he then handed to Albert. On entry Albert saw that the room was sparsely furnished. It contained a bed with a dull grey blanket, clean sheets and a pillow. There was a small bedside table on which was placed a bedside lamp. Next to the far wall was a plain wooden table. The two wooden drawers were empty save for a Bible. Minimal light was provided by a small square window which had a view of the rear of the premises.

'I hope you will be happy here Albert, and you will definitely be safer here than on that canal boat. At the moment you only have one neighbour in one of the adjoining rooms but you won't hear or have any trouble from that occupant.'

Albert thanked the priest and followed him back down the steps. At the foot of the stairs lay the exit to the outside world but there was another interior door which Father Michael opened. This led into a small dining room which contained a wooden table and four chairs. A sideboard stood against the wall. On the surface stood a basket of cutlery and a cruet set.

'This is where we will eat, Albert. The food is simple fare but sustaining. My living quarters are through that door over there,' pointing to a door on the far side of the table.

The Father and Albert retraced their steps and returned outside into the fresh air. Michael Creaney led Albert around the back of Albert's sleeping accommodation.

An expanse of ground had at one time been turned into a vegetable garden but was now untidy and overgrown with weeds. Down the side of the vegetable plot was a mesh fence behind which were four dog kennels.

There was only one occupant, a scruffy mixture of various breeds who yapped at them, as if in recognition.

'We only have one lodger at the moment' said Michael. 'The waifs and strays seem to find their way here. One of my parishioners, a butcher, supplies some scraps and the rest of their diet comes from the leftovers from our meal table. Some of the dogs are claimed and the others are taken to the dogs' home at Battersea.'

Both men returned to the dining room where they each took up occupancy of a plain wooden chair.

'Now Albert, we need to discuss the terms of your residency here at St Paul's. You will live here for free and you will eat with me here when you want to. As rent you will have to be prepared to do the odd menial task. I would like you to assume control of the vegetable garden and if any fresh vegetables are forthcoming we will regard it as a bonus.

'You will also take care of, and control any of the dogs in the kennels. Your own dog can be resident in that section and we will appoint him as leader of that area,' he said with a smile.

'I don't expect you to attend church. I am sure you will see the light eventually. My other small task for you is regarding the security of the church. On the odd occasion, especially when I have attended gatherings at the Plume of Feathers, I have been remiss when it comes to matters of securing God's house.'

Albert smiled.

'You will be responsible for locking up the church at night. That means clearing the vestibule of all customers who would have ambitions of spending the night sleeping on a cardboard bed inside the church. I know it sounds harsh but there are too many items of value in that sacred place. You will also be responsible for snuffing out the candles inside the church and in the vestibule as the local Fire Brigade Officer, who you will know from the Plume has advised me that it is a fire risk.'

'No problem Father. As soon as I can make arrangements with Nobby, I will ask him to help me move my stuff from the canal boat and I can pick up my dog Bart.'

'In the meantime Albert, we will have some soup and bread for lunch.'

As they sat at the table Albert heard a knock at the door and from the kitchen area emerged a woman, who Albert estimated was in her mid to late thirties.. She was slim and fairly tall, dressed in a plain grey skirt and black pullover. She wore a white blouse beneath her pullover. Her hair was cut short. She was not wearing any make-up and didn't wear any jewellery. Despite this, Albert was struck by her simple beauty. She possessed high cheekbones placed either side of an angular nose. Her short auburn hair was brushed back revealing beautiful green eyes.

The woman carried in a tray on which was placed two bowls of soup, a plate of dry pieces of bread and two soup spoons. She placed the tray on the table and without looking at either of the men, retired to the kitchen.

Michael Creaney noticed that Albert had been struck by the beauty of this woman.

'You've now met Helen. She has one of the rooms upstairs near your room. Some months ago Helen was a nun at that big convent in north London, the one near Finchley. She was dedicated to God, and to her vocation in life, but unfortunately her journey was derailed and she had to leave the convent. I found out that she originates from roughly the same part of Ireland as me and I made the decision to take her aboard here. She felt that she couldn't return to her native Ireland as she mistakenly thought that she had disgraced her family.'

'What happened Michael?' asked Albert.

'That's for another time and nothing you need to worry about, Albert. She works here as my housekeeper. She provides meals and cleans my room as well as the church. She does the odd bit of shopping and spends quite a bit of time in her room in a form of penitence. She also prays in the chapel frequently. She doesn't engage in conversation and keeps herself to herself. You need to give her some space, Albert, and respect her privacy.'

Albert nodded his consent and they supped their soup in silence.

11.

S Ted Fuller sat at his desk contemplating the way forward with his enquiry into the attempted murder of Albert Oxford. Oxford was no angel but he still deserved a rigorous investigation into the events that took place at the canal bank and in particular into the car which appeared to have been used in the commission of the crime.

The car was registered to William Cronk who had attempted to kill Oxford in Spain. Cronk thought he had been successful and then turned the gun on himself and was fatally wounded.

Fuller knew that Cronk had been working out of Southgate Police station before he retired. He had been investigating the murder of a young black girl, Marcia Williams, who had been working in McDonalds near Tottenham High Road.

Her death had happened because the young girl had been in the wrong place at the wrong time and the murder was as a result of tit-for-tat retaliations between rival gangs from north London and east London.

It had been thought that Oxford had been involved with others in the killing and disappearance of gang members in his part of east London. This had been done in retaliation due to frustration and the fact that nothing was being done by the local police to curb criminal activity. Oxford had not been charged with complicity as the case had been tainted by the involvement of two crooked CID officers who had both since died in a bizarre and shocking incident at Holborn Underground station.

Fuller rang Southgate Police station and asked the telephonist to be put through to the incident room. His call was answered by one of the police computer typists. Fuller identified himself and asked if there was anybody at the station who had worked with Cronk before he had retired. The young typist cupped her hand over the mouthpiece and signalled to Detective Sergeant Elaine Webster that there was a caller on the phone who she should speak to.

'DS Webster, how can I help you?'

'My name is DS Ted Fuller and I'm investigating the shooting of a man called Albert Oxford. I understand that Oxford was the subject of investigation by the late William Cronk and I'm looking to speak to someone who worked with or under Cronk.'

'I worked as his bag carrier for the last four years of his service. How can I help you?' asked Webster.

'You obviously know what happened in Spain. Can you tell me what happened to his assets and property after his suicide?'

'Yes, his house was left to his son who lives in Yorkshire. He came down to London and within a week he had had the house cleared and the property put on the market. It was advertised at a price that would ensure that it sold quickly.'

'What about the rest of his estate?' asked Fuller.

'Everything was left to his son, apart from two hundred pounds for a coffee machine in the major incident suite at Southgate Police station. He hated the old coffee machine. He reckons it was that machine and its contents that killed him.'

'Apart from the bullet through his brain you mean?'

'Sorry, I was referring to the cancer that ravaged his body.'

'What happened to his car?' asked Fuller.

'What do you mean?' asked Webster.

'At the time of his death he had a motor vehicle registered to his name and I was wondering where that vehicle is now' said Fuller.

'I'm afraid I can't help you with that,' replied Webster.

'Thank you for your help Sergeant Webster,' Fuller replied.

Detective Sergeant Webster picked up her mobile phone and texted a message:

Don't use transport. It's been compromised.

12.

ennis McMillan was getting dressed after his lunchtime tryst with Carmela. The small Spanish boutique hotel was a regular meeting place for McMillan and his girl-friend.

McMillan switched on his mobile phone and it pinged immediately with a flurry of messages and emails. He quickly scrolled through but one text message stood out:

Don't use transport. It's been compromised.

McMillan frowned. Cronk's car had been made available to him by Elaine Webster. He had picked it up after flying into London and had used it as a run-a-round whilst carrying out the intended execution of Albert Oxford. He thought he had been very careful with his use of the vehicle observing speed limits and cameras.

After he had shot Oxford he drove the vehicle to a multi-storey car park in Stratford where he had parked it on the uppermost floor. He had locked it and placed the weapon parts in a workmen's skip.

This message from Webster had worried him but when he tried to think about it rationally, he thought the chances of someone discovering the vehicle and its contents were very rare. Besides he had been meticulous in wiping and cleaning any trace of evidence.

Elaine Webster had been of valuable assistance to him. They shared the same hatred of Oxford who they held responsible for the death of their colleague, William Cronk.

13.

With Nobby's help, Albert had retrieved most of his important belongings including his radio. But most important of all, Albert had collected his dog Bart from the neighbouring canal boat owner. The dog had been overcome with excitement at seeing his master again.

Bart had now been placed in the dog-kennel area. Albert sat on a plain wooden bench contemplating what needed to be done with the garden area.

He had paid a visit to a local hardware shop and purchased various packets of seeds, mainly vegetables, and now gave some thought to a plan.

In the first instance he would have to cultivate the soil which involved digging hoeing and the removal of weeds.

After a couple of hours of toiling Albert sat down on the bench. He looked up at the window of his room. In the window of the adjoining apartment he thought he glimpsed someone watching him. Was it Helen or was it his imagination? He peered more closely but there was no one there.

Albert continued his work and after sowing the seeds, he marked what was planted. After watering them in, he fed the two occupants of the dog kennels.

After feeding the dogs Albert attached their two leads and took them to the green opposite the church.

At the evening meal which consisted of a meat stew accompanied by dry bread and a glass of water, Albert tried to catch the eye of Helen, but her head remained bowed and she entered and left in silence.

'I'm off to meet my flock,' the Father announced, 'would you care to join me Albert?'

'I would love to,' replied Albert, 'but first I need to make sure that Thomas is on sentry duty.'

Thomas Cannon was a retired army veteran who was classed as homeless. Because Father Creaney had extended kindness to him in the past regarding mental health issues Thomas had been indebted to the priest.

When the priest had asked him to be responsible for security measures at the church during pub opening hours, Thomas would sit at the back of the church silently thinking about his horrendous experiences in the deserts of the Middle East and remembering fallen comrades. The Middle East war had left its mark on Thomas Cannon.

When eventually the Father returned to the church, Thomas would slope off to his sheltered sparse accommodation in Stoke Newington.

When Michael Creaney and Albert returned to the church on this particular evening Albert went about his job of making sure the church was fire-proof. Thomas had only just left and Albert went to a side-room of the chapel and donned a monastic gown with hood as the church in the late evening had a cold feel about it.

Using his snuffer on an extended pole he walked up and down the aisles extinguishing the lit candles on their tall plinths. He extinguished the candles on the altar. His last job was to blow out the candles in the vestibule area and to kindly ask the carboarded occupants to vacate the premises.

Albert then closed the heavy oak doors and locked the church up. He retired to his room where his preferred habit was to listen to some classical music on his radio.

As he lay on his bed he contemplated his existence. His routine was simple and repetitive. Feeding and tending to the occupants of the kennels, opening up the church and lighting the main candles, a plain breakfast supplied by Helen followed by gardening, a simple lunch, some reading or listening to music, a frugal evening meal and then a drink in the Plume of Feathers. His last chore in the evening was to extinguish candles and lock up the church.

And, repeat.

Albert would have to think of a way to vary the routine. He had a plan.

14.

The restaurant was now empty of customers and Rafa was clearing away the last empty plates. He rearranged the chairs into their positions for the opening of business for the following day's trade.

Rafa had done well with the business, improving it from an ordinary street cafe up to a chic tapas restaurant which had a glowing reputation. This had been achieved by hard graft and the employment of a young and talented chef.

Alessandro, the chef, had left the premises to go home to his young wife and child.

Rafa was content with the restaurant apart from one thing. Profit margins were tight but any profit was obviated by the regular monthly visit by a gang member operating on behalf of the local hoodlum, El Caballo.

Rafa had been asked to contribute to the funds of El Caballo by paying a regular 300 Euros in exchange for the restaurant avoiding unnecessary accidents such as fire or vandalism. Rafa was expecting such a visit from one of El Caballo's henchmen.

He was just about to set the alarm and leave when a shadowy figure approached the restaurant door.

'*Tienes el dinero,*' (do you have the money)' he was asked.

'I have the money,' Rafa replied, 'but I need to pass on a message to your boss.'

'Money first and then you can tell me what your message is for *el jefe,* the boss.'

Rafa reluctantly handed over the Euros and took out his mobile phone. He scrolled through the photographs and showed the man a photo taken from the door of the restaurant leading to the car park. It showed a man escorting a very pretty lady to a car.

'Why would *el jefe* be interested in this?' asked the gangster.

'The woman in the photograph is El Caballo's daughter and I thought he would be interested in who she is associating with.'

The gangster pocketed Rafa's phone, something Rafa was not expecting.

'I can't operate this restaurant without that phone and I will have no means of contacting you or El Caballo if this man and his daughter come back to the restaurant.'

The gangster thought about this for a few seconds, took out his own mobile and took a screenshot of the incriminating image. He handed Rafa back his phone and said,

'You should expect a visit from my boss.'

15.

The young detective poked his head round the door of DS Ted Fuller's office,

'That car that you've flagged up has been sighted. The upper floor of a multi-storey car park in Stratford.'

Fuller grabbed his jacket and commandeered the young detective to drive him to the car park.

They drove up to the upper floor which was only occupied by three other cars. Fuller instructed the young detective to drive up to Cronk's car. A car park security officer in a hi-viz yellow jacket was standing next to the car.

'Is it locked? asked Fuller.

'Yep,' replied the attendant.

Fuller asked him and the young detective to tape-off the area containing the car with a notice left to say that this car was the subject of a police investigation.

Fuller made a phone call asking for a forensic team to attend after supplying them with the location.

Fuller noticed the presence of a security camera and obtained details of the operators which would allow him to view possible footage of the car and any occupants.

When the forensic operatives arrived, they donned

appropriate clothing and, wearing gloves, proceeded to examine the vehicle commencing with the outside of the car.

Fuller knew that this would take some time and dispatched his aide to purchase some coffee. Fuller looked round the floor of the car park. It seemed that the car had been deliberately placed at the furthest point from the camera.

The only other item that interested Fuller was a large skip which occupied a corner of this level of the car park and seemed to have been placed there as workmen had been working on an outside wall which looked as if it had been recently renovated and strengthened.

Fuller made a mental note to have it searched and instructed his detective after he returned with two polystyrene cups of lukewarm rancid coffee, to tape off the skip. This was also marked off as 'of police interest'.

On completing the examination of the vehicle's exterior the forensic duo turned their attention to the interior. The front passenger door was forced open. There was nothing of any interest on the inside of the vehicle and when the boot of the car was forced open, a similar sight greeted Fuller.

The scientists were left to dust and lift fingerprints. Fuller informed them that once they had completed that task they should arrange for the vehicle to be transported to the police compound in Hackney.

Back at the police station Fuller made an appointment with the operator who controlled the car park CCTV footage and later that afternoon visited their premises in Stratford.

He was shown to a wooden hard-backed chair in front of a bank of cameras. His host asked him if he could pinpoint a date or time and as Fuller knew the date of the shooting of Albert Oxford he was able to supply the operator with a narrow time-line.

The footage was easy to watch as there was minimal movement on the top floor of the car park. After thirty minutes Ted Fuller allowed himself to experience a frisson of excitement as he saw Cronk's vehicle drive into the car park.

The driver carefully manoeuvred the vehicle into the position where it had been found earlier.

Although the picture was dark and fuzzy, Fuller saw a figure emerge from the driver's side of the vehicle. He was hooded and of average height. Fuller thought him to be of stocky build. The figure then removed a package from the boot and took that package to the skip in the corner of the car park. He spent a bit of time appearing to hide or bury the package in the skip.

Fuller instructed the operator to make a copy of the clip and told him someone from his office would be with him the next day to take possession of the clip and to take a statement from him.

Fuller rang his forensic team and now instructed them to search the skip, informing them of the possibility of a package being secreted in the skip. He arranged to meet up with them later at Hackney Police station.

16.

Albert had decided he was going to have a day off from the garden. At the breakfast table Helen deposited a rack of warm toast and two mugs of coffee. Father Creaney looked bleary-eyed which Albert found unsurprising, considering the priest's capacity to consume pints of Guinness.

'I'm having a day off from the garden Father. I'm going to have a day of relaxation at the cricket down at Chelmsford. I should be back by late afternoon.'

'Albert, that sounds like a great idea. I don't know anything about cricket but the thought of a day sitting in the sunshine is very appealing. My flock will survive without me being on hand and Thomas can look after the building and the dogs.'

Helen looked at Albert with the merest trace of a smile but when Albert tried to catch her eye she quickly looked away. Albert couldn't believe how the hint of a smile had transformed her face into a thing of beauty.

Arrangements were made with Thomas regarding the security of the building. Thomas reassured them that the church was in a safe pair of hands.

Albert and the priest then made their way to Stratford rail

station by a short bus journey and Albert purchased their train tickets for the forty minute journey to Chelmsford.

Michael Creaney seemed excited by the prospect of the day out. On the journey to Chelmsford he sat at the window seat and marvelled at the countryside and the Essex villages flying past his window.

'Isn't it fascinating to be able to look into back gardens to see what people are doing with their lives? And aren't these villages beautiful? What a difference to where we are now in east London.'

'Do you miss Ireland at all, Michael?' asked Albert.

'I do Albert, it's very pretty and isolated. I do miss it. But there are a lot more souls to be saved in this part of the world.'

'Indeed,' replied Albert.

The rest of the journey was made in silence with Albert reading his purchased newspaper and Michael intently staring out of the carriage window taking in gardens with trampolines, tricycles, conservatories, barbecues and the occasional hot-tub.

When the train reached Chelmsford the carriage emptied, disgorging a crowd of flanneled supporters wearing white beanie sun-hats and carrying their lunch picnics.

Albert took Michael into the small supermarket just outside the station exit and purchased a bag of goodies for lunch consisting of a couple of meat pies, plastic-wrapped sandwiches and two plastic-bottled soft drinks. The pair then made their way down the hill towards the County Ground.

At the ground, Albert gained entry by a nod to an old acquaintance on the gate. His previous membership had stood him in good stead. Albert wondered what the gateman would have made of his travelling companion wearing his clerical collar under his light sports jacket.

Albert took the priest up to the upper tier of the small stand at the river end of the ground and they parked themselves on the white plastic seats.

Albert's timing had been well judged as both teams sauntered onto the pitch just after they had taken up occupancy.

'I'm looking forward to this Albert,' said the priest. 'Can you just run through the rules please?'

Albert looked at him in astonishment.

'Are you serious?'

Michael smiled at him.

Albert spent most of the next two hours explaining the simple basics of cricket and later went on to describe fielding positions and the difference between certain types of shot such as the backward defensive, the cover drive, the sweep shot and the leg glance.

'I love those fielding positions, Albert. Silly mid off, leg slip, long on. Who on earth made up those names?'

Nearing the luncheon interval the home team introduced their star spinner and Albert embarked on an effort to describe the difference between off spin and leg spin. Albert mentioned googlies, at which Michael burst out laughing.

'You wouldn't be winding me up, Albert?' asked the Father.

At this moment all the fielders raised their arms in an appeal to one of the white-coated umpires.

'What's happening there Albert?' asked the priest.

Albert rolled his eyes as he realised that a long explanation was again required of the laws of LBW. Michael appeared to absorb everything.

The umpires signalled the end of the morning session and the two teams left the ground and made their way towards the pavilion.

'Is that half-time Albert?' asked Michael.

'No, it's lunch Father. And later on this afternoon they will go off for twenty minutes for tea.'

'How civilised. What a great game this is. I wish I had discovered it earlier.'

The two cricketing companions opened up the purchased goods and partook of a pleasant lunch in the warm summer sunshine. Albert left his companion in his seat and after five minutes returned with two pints of beer in plastic glasses. A pint of Guinness for the preacher and a pint of Albert's favourite IPA bitter.

'This game of cricket just gets better and better' smiled the priest.

The players re-entered the arena and the game resumed at a sedate pace. Albert reflected on what a perfect day this had been so far.

Albert woke up with a start. He had fallen asleep and his head had been slumped onto his chest. He had dribbled onto his cotton shirt. He looked to his left and the Father was nowhere to be seen.

Albert walked up to the back of the stand where he had

a view of the hospitality area. Sitting at a table with three elderly men was Michael Creaney. They appeared to be in an excited animated conversation. Looking at the wooden trestle barbecue table it was obvious to Albert that a good few pints had been consumed.

Albert decided to leave them to it and he re-engaged with the cricket.

When Michael resumed his seat just before the tea interval he said to Albert,

'What a fantastic day and a fantastic sport Albert.'

'I saw you having a meaningful discussion with your three new friends' said Albert, noting the Father's ruddy complexion.

'Yes, I was just explaining to them the complications of the LBW rules' smiled the Father. 'Only kidding,' he added. 'We had a wide range of discussions talking about the pandemic, the vaccines, Brexit and the Government.'

'Must have been really interesting Father, but we need to consider catching the train back to east London as we wouldn't want to disappoint Helen.'

On the walk back up the hill to the train station Michael Creaney said to Albert,

'I've loved this day out. It's a wonderful thing, sport. It unites people and communities and one day soon I want to return the favour.'

'What do you mean Father?'

'I spend a lot of my spare time when I'm not at the Feathers, at Shoreditch Boys boxing club. The noble art, as it is sometimes called, plays a huge part in keeping young boys on the straight and narrow. It teaches them to defend themselves and promotes healthy competition. I enjoy my visits to their gymnasium and I have followed the paths of some kids who have become very good boxers. I insist that one day you will come with me to Shoreditch and when the opportunity presents itself I'll take you as my guest to York Hall to watch a programme of boxing.'

Albert was aware of York Hall which was a famous East London venue used mainly for boxing promotions.

'I would very much like that' said Albert.

They arrived at the station. When the train pulled into the station they were able to find two seats together. Father Creaney slept for the entire return journey on the train.

Back at the church Helen served their frugal meal of meat and potatoes.

'You've caught the sun' she said to Father Creaney in a quiet voice with a soft Irish accent.

This was the first time Albert had heard her voice and it added to the list of qualities that he found attractive in the woman.

'Yes,' said the Father, 'Albert and I have been to see a game of cricket. It was fascinating.'

Albert smiled, wondering to himself how much the bar area at the ground had added to the enjoyment of Michael's day.

'Did your team win?' asked Helen, of Albert.

'No, this particular game is played over four days' he replied.

'Even then it could be a draw,' interjected Father Creaney who was now suddenly an expert on the game. Albert smiled.

When Helen retired to the kitchen area Father Creaney said to Albert,

'She doesn't know a lot about cricket, that poor girl.'

Albert smiled again and gave thought to the prospect of listening to the priest summarising the day's play on future editions of 'Test Match Special' on Radio Four.

17.

etective Sergeant Elaine Webster tied up her black Labrador to the harness in the rear of her Ford estate car and drove towards Hackney Marshes. She parked in the car park near the changing rooms. Unclipping her dog she kept him on the extended leash and strode towards the River Lea Navigation canal.

Both towpaths were busy and Webster had to cross a footbridge to reach the side of the canal that she required access to. Once there, she walked the dog towards where Albert Oxford's canal boat had been moored. She saw the evidence of the incident in the form of remnants of a length of brightly coloured police tape fluttering from the trunk of a tree.

Slowing her pace, Webster noticed that the occupants of a canal boat were on the deck of their bright red and green boat. A man dressed in dungarees and trainers had a pot of green paint in his hand and was touching up parts of the livery with a brush. He occasionally paused to admire his handiwork.

A woman was tending to potted plants on the deck and generally tidying up the deck with a broom.

'Good morning,' Webster called out to the couple, 'what a lovely day.'

Both looked up from their respective tasks and smiled at Webster, although Webster was under the impression that the smiles were meant for her black Labrador and not her.

'You look busy,' said Elaine Webster.

'Not really,' said the man putting down his paintbrush and savouring a break in the repetitive routine of applying paint to wood.

'We touch up the paintwork twice a year to keep her looking okay.'

'What's happened to the nice man with the Jack Russell that was in the boat next to you. I haven't seen him for a while.'

'Didn't you hear?' said the woman. 'He was involved in a shooting and they thought he had died.'

'Oh my goodness,' exclaimed Webster, 'I didn't know. Is he okay?'

'He was in hospital for a few days but he's fine now. He's been down to collect his dog.'

'And is he not living here anymore?' asked Webster.

'No, he is staying with an Irish priest somewhere in Hackney or Stoke Newington.'

Webster caught sight of the man frowning at the woman.

'If you see him, will you pass on my best wishes,' said Webster.

'We will,' said the man. 'Can I say who was asking after him?'

'He wouldn't know me' said Webster, 'but we had a

mutual acquaintance. Do you know which church he's resident at?'

The man looked at his partner and then said to Webster, 'I'm sorry, we don't know.'

'Thanks, pass on my best wishes and hope to see him soon.'

'We will.'

Webster returned to her car and after securing the dog in the back of the car sat in the driver's seat of her car and took out her mobile phone and started a comprehensive search of churches in the Hackney and Stoke Newington area. The search would require certain parameters that had to include living accommodation.

Webster concluded that the best place to conduct the search on her mobile phone would be in the comfort of her living room with a glass of chilled white wine as her companion.

She drove off towards home satisfied with her enquiries.

18.

Albert Oxford lay on his bed with his hands behind his head. He contemplated where he was at on the cycle of his life. He enjoyed his lifestyle, working in the vegetable garden, doing the odd menial job concerning the church that Father Creaney asked him to do.

He had the occasional night out down at the Plume of Feathers and had visited the Shoreditch Boys boxing club with Father Creaney. After nights at the Plume he was able to steer the priest home after his consumption of copious pints of the black stuff.

He managed to get out for a day's cricket every now and then and on his return was quizzed by Father Creaney as to the score. Albert was convinced that his imparted information about the state of the current game flew way above Michael's head.

The frugal meals were served at the table by Helen who did not join them but ate her food separately in the kitchen area. Any attempt to catch Helen's eye was met with a downward glance but Albert had been sure that on more than one occasion he had spotted Helen observing him from her room when he was at work in the garden.

Helen would also supply scraps of food for the dogs in the kennels and it appeared that she had a soft spot for Bart, Albert's Jack Russell.

Albert's attempts to engage with Helen had not met with any success apart from the return of pleasantries exchanged before meals served at the table. Helen avoided eye contact with Michael and Albert but there had appeared the faintest trace of a smile when Michael and Albert had discussed the game of cricket that Albert had attended and Michael went on to speak as if he was a leading exponent of the game.

When Albert handed over produce from the garden to supplement the meals he was thanked by a nod of the head which then looked towards the floor to avoid eye contact.

Albert had made friends with Thomas, the custodian of the church through the day. Thomas on occasions would help Albert with the heavy digging and lifting. Every now and then Albert would produce a couple of cans of beer which they would consume after hard toil. They sat on an old wooden bench at the edge of the vegetable plot and fruit bushes.

Albert discovered after gentle coaxing, that Thomas had been in the Armed Forces for about ten years serving in the Middle East amongst other places. He had been pensioned off by the Army suffering from post traumatic stress and like many of his companions had been abandoned by the Army and the government to fend for themselves.

Thomas was officially homeless and had slept rough for months until he had been pointed out to Father Creaney by one of the priest's flock. The Father offered Thomas the job of being 'front of house' at the church doors in return for food. Thomas would spend most of his day just inside the large doors of the church except for the occasional sojourn to help Albert, and to sit with him after their gardening tasks.

Father Creaney had also found Thomas very basic sleeping accommodation at a homeless shelter within the borough.

It was obvious to Albert that Thomas held the priest in high regard and would do anything to protect him.

Despite the fact that Father Creaney was partial to a glass or two of Guinness, he was a very busy priest and took his pastoral work seriously. He took mass, undertook baptisms, the occasional marriage and was to be seen popping into the confessional box to listen to the failings and admissions of his flock. Albert could see that he was respected and loved by his regular church-goers who didn't seem to mind his idiosyncratic life-style.

Life was meandering on in the slow lane. Albert didn't mind that at all, but that was about to change.

19.

Once a fortnight, Helen left the church to walk to the library in Stoke Newington High Street. The books that she borrowed were read avidly and always returned on time.

She stood out in the grey miserable weather due to the bright yellow anorak she was wearing. Because of the threat of rain she wore the hood up and took her usual route which involved the side streets of Hackney and Stoke Newington.

Just as she was about to emerge onto the High Street she became aware that two youths on bicycles had ridden past her but had suddenly turned round and were now approaching her from behind.

Alarmed, she clutched her shoulder bag tightly but the youth who was nearest to her drew up alongside her and punched her in the face. She yelled out in pain. The second youth grabbed her shoulder bag and viciously pulled it from her grip and, with their spoils, the two youths cycled off furiously in the direction of the High Street.

Helen was upset at the loss of her bag as not only did it contain her library books, but her purse contained a photograph of her parents. The purse also had a small amount of money which Helen had intended to use for the purchase of groceries.

The punch to her face had hurt her and she decided that her best course of action was to return to the church. She retraced her steps and on reaching the chapel the first person she saw was Thomas, who was sitting just inside the door of the church.

Thomas saw immediately that she was distressed and could plainly see the purple bruise on her left cheekbone. Thomas shouted out to Albert who was working in the garden.

Albert rushed to the front of the chapel alarmed by the urgency in Thomas's cry for assistance. He could see that the ex-nun was very upset. He got a glass of water from the kitchen which he proffered to Helen. She accepted with thanks and Albert asked her to tell him what happened.

She repeated the story but got upset when describing the contents of her bag.

'I had a photograph of my mother and father. Daddy passed away two years ago and it is the only photograph I have of them. I carry it everywhere.'

Albert asked Helen if she wanted to be checked over at the hospital but she politely declined. He also asked her for a description as best as she could give, but understood when she was a bit vague with descriptions. However, she was able to give a description of a cycle with its red markings and brand name, '*Trek*'.

As Helen was regaining her composure, the figure of Father Creaney strode into view. Albert very quickly acquainted him with what had happened. The priest was upset and said to Helen,

'Helen, Albert and I will take care of our own feeding arrangements this evening. I suggest you retire to your room to rest and recuperate'.

Helen thanked him and retired to her quarters still visibly upset.

'I've some work to do in the chapel this afternoon,' said Father Creaney, 'and afterwards I shall take sustenance aboard at the Plume of Feathers. Would either of you care to accompany me to the public house,' asked Michael.

'I've got a little job to do,' said Thomas, 'and I'll need the assistance of Albert, if you don't mind. It means that there'll be nobody here until we get back, but, if you're in the chapel perhaps you'll forgive my absence for a couple of hours?'

Father Creaney eyed the pair of them suspiciously but gave his assent.

'Don't get into any trouble,boys,' he added.

'Right Albert, you can come with me if you like. I'm capable of doing this on my own but it's up to you.'

'I wouldn't miss this for the world,' replied Albert.

They set off on foot without much conversation. When they reached the High Street, Thomas looked up and down the street.

Spotting something about 200 yards away, Thomas set off in that direction, closely followed by Albert.

In an abandoned shop doorway was a human form, huddling and covered in a blanket, sitting on a few layers of cardboard.

'Brendan, good afternoon. I need a little bit of help,' Thomas said to the man.

The bearded, unkempt face looked up and said,

'Is that you, Tom? Where are you hiding these days?'

'Not far away Bren. I need your help. A mate of ours has just been mugged. They nicked her bag which contained something very personal to her. One of them was on a red Trek bike.'

'Albanians,' replied Brendan. 'This area round here is infested with them. A law unto themselves. They think they can do what they want. No police presence. A half decent flamethrower would sort the problem.'

Thomas smiled. His memories of working alongside Brendan in a hot foreign country would always remain with him. They had looked after each other and their small team of highly trained operatives had caused havoc amongst the opposition.

Brendan was now uncared for, an unwanted veteran, abandoned by successive governments and left to fend for himself in shop doorways. Thomas had considered himself lucky that Father Creaney had thrown him a lifeline. Thomas was bitter that all these good men had been thrown on the scrap heap whilst migrants from foreign lands were wading ashore on the south coast and being feted by the government.

'Where should I aim the flamethrower, Brendan?' asked Thomas.

'You could start with a cafe they use in Spring Terrace. It's about half a mile from here. You can't miss it. It sits back off the road. A lot of them use it. They sling their bikes down on the pavement and everyone has to walk around them. An old boy nearly got knocked down by a bus the other week.'

'Thanks Brendan. I'll pop back and see you when I've finished with this.'

Albert nodded to Brendan and followed Thomas in the direction of Spring Terrace.

Next to an Estate Agents office was a cafe which did indeed sit back off the road. Loud music poured out of the street door.

Albert looked at six bicycles littering the pavement. He caught Thomas's eye and pointed at a red Trek bike.

Thomas nodded. He approached the bike and stood on every spoke of the rear wheel. He stamped hard until every spoke on the frame had been grotesquely bent.

Thomas then guided Albert across the road where they took up a position behind the metal gate guarding the entrance of a building site. They had a perfect view of the front of the cafe.

After some thirty minutes, four youths wearing dark hoodies emerged from the cafe. The owner of the Trek bicycle shouted out loudly when seeing the state of his bike. The other three laughed, picked up their bikes and cycled off leaving their companion mournfully rueing the end of his cycling career.

Thomas picked up a short scaffolding pole from the ground of the building site and with Albert he crossed the road to where the hoodie was standing over his bike.

Thomas approached the youth concealing the scaffold pole behind his back.

'What's your name, pal?' asked Thomas.

'Who wants to know?' replied the scrawny youth with a sneer.

Thomas produced the scaffold pole from behind his back and repeated his question.

'My name is Moro,' replied the youth.

'Okay, Moro, what hospital do you want to attend?' asked Thomas.

Moro screwed his face inquisitively, intimating that he didn't understand the question.

'Okay, let's try another line. Mortuary or intensive care unit?'

'Burial or cremation?' chipped in Albert.

'You need to think carefully about the next question as it'll decide which hospital will be treating you,' said Thomas.

'You, and a mate of yours robbed a lady this afternoon. What did you do with the backpack you stole from her?'

'I don't know what you're talking about,' he replied.

'Homerton Hospital it is then,' and with that, Thomas smashed the scaffolding pole into Moro's left knee cap causing him to scream out in pain.

'Wrong answer,' said Thomas, 'you have one more attempt and then it'll be your other knee followed by your ankles. Do you understand?' he asked.

'You're a fucking mad person,' said Moro, which was obviously not the answer Thomas was hoping for. He raised the pole to strike again but the youth raised his arms in self defence and shouted out,

'Okay, what do you want to know,' he pleaded.

'What did you do with the woman's bag after you nicked the money out of her purse?'

'The bag is in a waste bin just inside the park.'

Thomas and Albert set off for Clissold Park but before leaving the youth Thomas left Moro with a parting shot on Moro's ankle bone.

'If I don't find the bag, I will come back after you,' He threw the scaffolding pole at the youth, striking him with a glancing blow on the head.

'Well done, Thomas,' said Albert, 'I was most impressed with your interrogation techniques.'

'Basic stuff Albert, the Albanians are lacking in moral fibre. They wouldn't last a minute in a real fight.'

They arrived at the entrance to Clissold Park and Albert spotted a waste bin beside a clump of bushes. Fortunately, nothing of any note had been added to the bin since Helen's bag had been deposited.

Albert retrieved the bag and was pleased to see that it contained three library books and a brown leather purse. All the notes and loose coins had been removed from the purse, but Albert was pleased to see that a small photograph was still tucked away in one of the envelope compartments. The photograph showed an elderly couple standing by a farmyard gate.

On their return to the church they made a detour to where they had last seen Brendan.

'Thanks Brendan,' said Albert, pressing a ten pound note into his hand. Brendan slipped the note into his trouser pocket.

As they entered the driveway of the church they were

met by Father Creaney. Albert raised the bag and purse as a returning knight would hold aloft the spoils of war. Father Michael beamed a huge smile.

'I hope you didn't need to resort to your old SAS skills?' asked the Father.

Thomas frowned at the priest's indiscretion and he noticed that Albert raised an eyebrow in interest.

'Sorry Thomas, that was quite inappropriate on my part.'

All three men retired to the kitchen area of the priest's quarters and sat at the long wooden table. Thomas got up to make a pot of tea for the three of them but just as he picked up the kettle, Helen entered the room and frowned at Thomas in admonishment as she deemed that he was interfering in her catering duties.

Apart from the semblance of a frown Albert saw that her face was expressionless until she noticed her backpack on the kitchen table. She looked at the bag and permitted herself a smile. Albert thought her smile to be one of the most beautiful things he had seen in a fellow human being.

Helen picked up her bag and, ignoring the books, carefully opened the purse. Another glorious smile radiated the room as she found the photograph of her parents which she held to her cheek. She kissed the photograph.

After making tea, Helen scooped up her bag and contents and retired to her room.

'Your little venture this afternoon boys was worth whatever you did, just for that smile,' said Father Creaney. 'I've never seen her smile until now. And please spare me the details of what you did. I've a weak constitution.'

'I'll see you in the confessional box later in the week,' said Thomas.

All three men laughed.

20.

In her free days when Detective Sergeant Elaine Webster was not working out of the Major Enquiry office at Southgate Police station she could be found pounding the streets of Hackney and Stoke Newington.

Her mission was to find Albert Oxford. She had felt cheated when Oxford had avoided execution by Dennis McMillan. She and McMillan had been close friends of William Cronk who had committed suicide after another failed attempt on Albert Oxford's life.

Webster had discovered that Oxford was living under the same roof as a priest at a church in the Hackney or Stoke Newington area. Her search so far had proved fruitless and had taken up four of her days when not at work. No matter, she thought. All this walking was keeping her fit.

The next church on Webster's list was the Catholic church of St. Paul. When she stopped outside the church she could see from the wooden notice board that the incumbent priest was listed as a Father Michel Creaney.

The large front doors to the church were open and Webster ventured inside. She sat at one of the pews as if in sober contemplation and slowly looked round. A priest with a florid face approached her and, in a soft Irish accent, asked her if she needed any assistance. Declining his polite offer, Webster went to leave the church. She passed Thomas Cannon sitting in his customary position in the vestibule. He was reading a book.

Outside in the fresh air Webster was about to walk back onto the street when she heard the sound of dogs barking. As she looked down the alleyway she saw a dog compound with two occupants arguing over a plastic toy. She noted that one of the dogs was a Jack Russell.

Webster retraced her steps and approached Thomas in the vestibule.

'Those two dogs outside. Are they strays?' asked Webster.

'Only one of them,' replied Thomas.

'The Jack Russell is so cute. Is there any chance he would be available for adoption?' enquired Webster.

'You're out of luck, lady. That one belongs to Albert.'

'Oh, that's a shame,' said Webster, trying her utmost to contain her glee.

21.

Detective Sergeant Ted Fuller had received the predictable news that the rifle found in the skip at the Stratford multi-storey car park had come back clean with absolutely no clues to be gleaned.

However, he had allowed himself to get excited about the news of a significant fingerprint found on the inside of the boot of the car. Other fingerprints had been found but were located in run-of-the-mill places where fingerprints would be expected to be found.

To eliminate the fingerprints of the owner of the car, the deceased William Cronk, the Fingerprint Department had searched an index of serving police officers and this index also included a list of retired officers. Fuller knew that this index existed as new recruits were obliged to supply their fingerprints to assist forensic scientists eliminate the fingerprints of police officers legitimately at the scenes of crime.

The significant fingerprint found in the boot of the car belonged to Dennis Charles McMillan, a Detective Sergeant who had retired early in his career. Other fingerprints found included those of Detective Sergeant Elaine Webster and William Cronk himself.

Fuller decided it was time to pay Webster a visit.

Fuller drove his car to Southgate Police station hoping his drive was not going to be fruitless. At reception he asked for Detective Sergeant Webster, stating his own name and rank and producing his warrant card. Two minutes later Webster appeared at the front desk and pressed a buzzer which allowed Fuller to enter the confines of the station.

'To what do I have this pleasure,' asked Webster.

'I need to have a little chat with you and I thought it would be better for both of us if it was done face-to-face rather than over the telephone,' said Fuller.

A concerned frown creased Webster's face. She led him down a corridor and up a flight of stairs and then into a room which was sparsely furnished and contained a wooden table and four chairs. On the table there was recording equipment with a microphone and cassette recorder.

They were in one of the rooms used for official interviews but Fuller said,

'We won't be needing that,' pointing at the equipment.'

'I should hope not,' replied Webster.

'Maybe later, but let me tell you what I've got,' said Fuller. He let that sink in.

'As you know I'm investigating the shooting of a man called Albert Oxford. The car used to convey the shooter away from the scene of the crime is registered to the late William Cronk, your old boss. The car has been discovered in a multi-storey car-park and a weapon discovered in the close proximity.'

'Why exactly do you want to speak to me about it?' asked Webster.

'The Fingerprint Department has furnished me with the details of people whose fingerprints were found in the forensic search of the car. They include the fingerprints of Cronk and yourself.'

Webster appeared to consider her reply.

'Cronk's fingerprints will obviously be in the car somewhere. As far as I was concerned I'd obviously been in William's car on numerous occasions through the course of our work and also socially.'

'Socially?' asked Fuller.

'We occasionally went out for a social drink together. Nothing else, just a drink. He was delightful company until he became ill. His mind turned a little bit towards the end.'

'Another interesting print was found in the car,' said Fuller. 'It belongs to a retired police officer called Dennis Charles McMillan.'

Webster would have made a good poker player as there wasn't a flicker of interest at the mention of that name.

'I can't say the name means anything to me,' replied Webster.

'I thought Cronk might have mentioned him,' said Fuller, 'they were good mates and played rugby together.'

'That might explain why his fingerprint was in the car then,' said Webster.

'Indeed it might.'

'Was anything found on the weapon?' asked Webster.

'Unfortunately not,' replied Fuller.

'I'm sorry that I can't help you anymore. If I remember anything about this McMillan I will give you a call.'

Fuller stood up to leave. Webster escorted him back down to ground level.

Before leaving Fuller thanked Webster for her time but on walking back to his car he felt uncomfortable about Detective Sergeant Webster. There was something about her that left a bad taste in his mouth.

Fuller returned to his office and made a couple of telephone enquiries and delved into his computer to confirm what he had been told on the telephone.

He had established that Dennis McMillan was in receipt of a police pension, albeit that it wasn't a full service pension, and that the pension was paid into a Spanish Post office situated in a small Spanish town. The Correos, or Post Office, received McMillan's pension once a month and had done so for the last eight years.

Fuller was able to establish with another phone call details of McMillan's service record. This interested Fuller as it showed that McMillan had worked with the Firearms Section at New Scotland Yard.

All very interesting but Fuller did not have enough on McMillan to justify a trip to Spain. He would have to think about how he was going to handle this.

Elaine Webster typed out a message on her mobile phone:

F/P's found in vehicle. Nothing to worry about. Nil on weapon. Have located AO. E59JM.

She pressed 'send' and would then wait to hear from the recipient.

Webster was just slightly concerned about her visit from Fuller but, having thought it through, decided that there was nothing to get over-worried about. She would carry on as normal. Her involvement was at an end. McMillan would take care of Oxford and William Cronk's final mission in life would have been completed.

22.

ennis McMillan sat in his office contemplating his plans for the day. He had two assignments lined up. One was pleasurable and one was work related.

The first task was to take out his young beautiful girlfriend Carmela for a spot of lunch. This would hopefully be followed by a visit to a hotel-room which they had used before to satisfy their cravings.

McMillan knew he was the big beneficiary in this relationship as he considered himself punching above his body weight with a young woman who would look classy on anybody's arm. He did remind himself that he frequently showered expensive gifts on Carmela and that they only drank the finest wines and champagnes. The hotel room was always at the best hotel in that part of Spain and meals were always of the highest quality.

These habits of course, did not come cheaply which was the reason McMillan was pleased that his illegal sorties with Mateo paid very well. His regular boat trips went a long way to financing his lifestyle and, although there was a high element of risk involved, McMillan was prepared to take that chance.

He had never shrank from a challenge whilst employed by the Metropolitan Police, even if that bravado had ultimately cut short his police career.

Carmela had seemed to enjoy the small chic restaurant they had been to recently, so the plan was to revisit that location again for lunch. It was quiet and they were usually given a table away from the large bay window and restaurant door.

McMillan's second task was to enable him to keep his financial situation fluid. He would steer his motor-boat with Mateo aboard, to the predestined spot in the Mediterranean where they would pick up a package of grade A drugs. Mateo was ultimately responsible for taking the package to one of Costa Blanca's drug overlords. McMillan's share was most welcome and was worth all the hassle of the subterfuge.

But, first things first. McMillan drove to the point where he said he would meet Carmela. She jumped into the passenger seat of his saloon, flicked back her long unnaturally blond hair and gave McMillan the benefit of one of her most seductive smiles.

When they arrived at the restaurant, McMillan parked his car below the shade of one of the many trees at the edge of the car park.

They were met at the restaurant door by Rafa who showed them to the table that they usually sat at. He left them to settle and reappeared with a menu and wine list. Rafa retired to the bar area whilst they both considered what fare they were going to order.

McMillan was quite happy for Carmela to choose as his

mind kept straying to the prospects facing him at the hotel room later in the afternoon.

Meanwhile, behind the cover of the optics and bottles of liqueurs, Rafa sent a message to an associate of El Caballo that the couple he was interested in had just sat down for lunch.

When Carmela and her beau had finished lunch, McMillan asked for the bill. The substantial bill was settled. They were thanked personally by Rafa and escorted to the door.

McMillan and Carmela walked to McMillan's car, unaware that they were being watched by the occupants of two other vehicles.

El Caballo, the Horse, watched them with disbelief. He saw that his beloved daughter was walking arm-in-arm with one of the people he hated most, McMillan, El Ingles.

The Horse had to think quickly. He didn't want his daughter endangered in any way and he had to be very careful with McMillan. He knew that McMillan was responsible for the supply of drugs to a high-profile drugs baron further down the coast. If he got rid of McMillan he risked incurring the wrath of the baron and that would obviously cause him trouble which he didn't want. The drug baron was higher up the pay scale than El Caballo.

Sitting in the next car to El Caballo was his trusty lieutenant El Nariz, The Nose, so named due to the ultra prominent feature on the front of his face.

El Nariz was instructed to follow McMillan and El Caballo's daughter and report back to him.

Later that day, when McMillan and Carmelo were

frolicking in a bedroom at the Santa Cristina boutique hotel, El Nariz phoned his boss and told him the news he probably did not want to hear. Controlling his rage, he gave serious thought to his predicament. He had to find a way round this.

El Caballo instructed The Nose to follow McMillan once they had finished whatever they were doing. El Caballo winced at the thought. He also instructed two of his motor bike team to assist El Nariz.

El Caballo did not hear from his henchman until the next morning when he appeared at his villa.

The Nose informed him that they had followed McMillan who had dropped Carmela off at her apartment. McMillan had then driven to the dock area where he had met up with another man. Both men got into McMillan's motor boat and they had motored off into the darkening sky.

El Nariz knew that he would be expected to await the return of McMillan and his partner. He and the two bike riders placed themselves to await such a return.

Some five hours later, El Nariz heard the chugging of the small engine of a motor boat and saw that it was, indeed, the return of McMillan and his compatriot. Nariz watched as the small craft moored up on the opposite side of the dock and saw both men manhandle a large package wrapped in waterproof plastic into the back of a fish market van which was driven away by the younger of the two men.

One of the bikes was instructed to follow the van and the other bike rider was instructed to follow McMillan.

At Caballo's villa, El Nariz updated his boss. The fish van went to an address that El Caballo knew was close to the home of the drug boss.

After the package had been deposited there, the bike rider had followed the fish-van driver back to an address in the village.

The other bike rider reported that McMillan had returned to an address which appeared to be where McMillan resided.

23.

Bart, the Jack Russell belonging to Albert, had been joined by another canine companion in the kennels. He was a smooth-coated mongrel descended from many different breeds and was very boisterous.

He was one of many strays that over the course of the years had found its way to the kennels at the chapel where it would be cared for before either being claimed or moved on to Battersea Dogs Home.

After his stint in the garden during the morning, Albert would take Bart and any other lodgers from the kennels on a walk to the park about three-quarters of a mile away from the church.

Albert knew he would have a struggle containing the black mongrel as well as his own dog so was pleasantly surprised when Helen appeared at the rear kitchen door.

'Will you need a hand with that other dog?' she asked.

'That would be very nice of you,' replied Albert, and with that, Helen went upstairs to her room and reappeared wearing her bright yellow cagoule.

'It'll be best if you take the small dog and I'll take care of this big bag of hair,' said Albert.

Albert handed over Bart's leash, with Bart attached. He happily wagged his tail at the prospect of a walk to a local park.

The walk was made in silence but Albert could see that Helen's demeanour was brighter than usual and instead of her customary downward gaze she appeared to be enjoying the walk in the warm summer afternoon temperature.

Once they had reached the park, Bart was released to run freely but Albert kept the other dog on its lead.

'I can't run the risk of him running away again,' said Albert, 'that's how we have inherited him.'

Albert produced a scruffy tennis ball from his pocket and while Helen held on to the mongrel Albert threw the ball for Bart to chase. Helen laughed out loudly at the sight of this little bundle scampering at break-neck speed in pursuit of the ball.

Albert had already been smitten by her smile and now her laugh made her even more a vision of beauty.

They sat at a park bench seat and whilst Helen looked after both dogs, Albert disappeared and a short while later returned with two polystyrene cups of tea which had been purchased from a burger van on the edge of the park.

'Father Michael has this wonderful trait of collecting waifs and strays,' said Albert, 'and not just the dogs. Thomas and myself also fit into this category.'

Helen did not reply but sat sipping her tea through the plastic lid and looking at the ground.

'Can I ask you, Helen, how you finished up at St Pauls?'

'It's not something I want to talk about. Maybe another time. But I can say that I also fit into the category of waifs and strays.'

After they had finished their tea and disposed of the cups they made their way in silence back to the church. Albert placed both dogs in the kennels.

'Thank you,' said Helen. 'I enjoyed our walk.'

'Not a problem,' said Albert, 'perhaps we can do it again on a more regular basis?'

'I would like that,' she replied.

Later that afternoon, Albert sat down at the long wooden table with Father Michael Creaney. Helen entered carrying a tray with two steaming bowls of soup and two wedges of plain white bread. Helen gave both men the merest trace of a smile and then retired back to the kitchen.

Michael looked at Albert and with a raised eyebrow said,

'Tell me I'm not imagining things Albert. Helen's mood seems to have lifted. Her smile lights the room. I wonder what's going on in that pretty head?'

'She came out for a walk with me this afternoon. We took the two dogs to the park. She volunteered and seemed to enjoy the fresh air and the walk.'

For the second time in as many minutes the Father raised an eyebrow and then smiled.

'I'm pleased she's coming out of her shell a little bit. She needs to be treated with kid gloves, Albert. She's a very sensitive soul and I hope that this is the start of her recovery process.'

'Can I ask what Helen is recovering from Father?'

'As you probably know Albert, she was a nun at the big convent in Finchley. She arrived from a little village in Ireland as one of life's innocents and she is still that sweet innocent person. When these young ladies become nuns, they dedicate their lives completely to God, and everything they do involves God, either in prayer or whatever they do through the day and night.

'Unfortunately for Helen, one of the visiting priests to the convent was a handsome young man, a bit like myself,' he smiled, 'but without the toupee.'

Albert laughed.

'Helen unfortunately found that she had feelings for the young priest and tried everything in her power to control her emotions. When the Mother Superior questioned her, she admitted to the Mother that her emotions were all over the place. She was destroyed. Mother Superior spoke to me. She told me the woman couldn't go back to her village in Ireland as she felt she had disgraced her family. I volunteered to take Helen into St Pauls and the rest, as they say, is history.'

'What a shame,' said Albert, 'she's still got a life to lead and I hope she finds some happiness.'

'I'll drink to that,' said the priest, 'and that's where I'm heading off to now. Would you fancy a pint of Guinness, Albert, or will you stick to that unholy stuff you call beer?'

'Thank you Father, I'll join you. It'll give me a chance to catch up with Nobby and the others.'

Both men sauntered down to the Plume of Feathers, safe in the knowledge that Thomas was managing front-of-house. All Albert had to worry about was to ensure that he was back in good time to snuff out the lit candles and to lock up the premises.

24.

Carlos, El Caballo, wrestled with a problem which had caused him the odd sleepless night.

His beautiful daughter Carmela, was cavorting with a man called Dennis McMillan. McMillan had supplied evidence of Horse's infidelity which had led to the divorce of El Cabello and his ex-wife, the mother of Carmela.

El Caballo hated McMillan with a passion and was determined to cause him extreme harm. The only problem was that he now knew that McMillan was the main facilitator in the supply of top grade drugs to the drug overlord who happened to be a few pay scales above El Caballo in the pecking order of criminal masters in that part of Spain.

The Horse knew that before he took revenge on McMillan he would have to square it with El Poderoso, 'The Powerful'.

El Caballo ordered one of his most trusty henchmen to arrange a meeting with El Poderoso and the following day El Caballo was driven to a disused retail factory site on the outskirts of a mountain Spanish village near to where the drug overlord lived.

The two cars containing El Caballo and his henchmen,

who were there to provide protection for their boss, drove through broken down wire gates hanging off their hinges into a huge dustbowl of a yard.

The two cars came to a stop in the middle of this space. Looking out of his rear-seat passenger window El Caballo saw that all the buildings on the perimeter of the square were no longer in use. The whitewash had long since faded and had been replaced by streaky brown stains caused by rain. The Horse could see that many of the windows contained shadowy figures who he quite rightly recognised as belonging to El Poderosos's team.

A diminutive figure appeared from a doorway. Although El Caballo had not set eyes on his opponent for a number of years, he was still instantly recognisable. Short in stature and wafer-thin, he would not have given anyone the impression that he controlled most of the organised crime in this part of Spain. The facial features were a collection of points, pointed ears, pointed nose, thin narrow face, wispy dyed black hair. He wore dark Levi denim jeans, a light brown leather jacket and brown leather cuban-heeled boots that made him taller than he actually was. He wore his trademark scarf made of the finest wool from the Spanish Merino sheep. It was light blue in colour and it was rumoured that he wore it to conceal hideous wounds on his neck.

El Poderoso stood his ground. El Caballo exited the car and approached him. They stood facing each other two yards apart. Caballo nodded at him and got a nod back in return.

El Poderoso turned on his heel and returned through the

door he had emerged from. El Caballo followed him.

Inside the room dust had gathered on broken-down machinery equipment. Two plain wooden hard-backed chairs faced each other. Both men sat down and talked.

Later that afternoon as El Caballo was being returned to his village, he reflected on the meeting with El Poderoso. Caballo had expressed his wish to remove McMillan from the scene and gave the reasons why. He acknowledged that McMillan played a role in El Poderoso's drug operation. The matters were discussed in an unfriendly manner, with the upshot being that if El Poderoso's operation was not compromised in any way, then he would give his blessing to El Caballo to do what he wanted with McMillan.

El Caballo now had to ponder over the best way to replace McMillan in the chain of movement. He knew that McMillan had a trip out to sea on his motorboat every fortnight or so, and that he was accompanied by another man who assisted him in this operation. The key would be for this other person to assume control of this operation and then McMillan would become superfluous to this operation. Plenty to think about.

On return to his villa, El Caballo called a meeting of six of his most trusted henchmen. He explained what had taken place and tasked his crew with finding out who was McMillan's aide. Their job would be to identify him, where he lived, and find out every detail about his family and background. This would allow El Caballo's gang to exert undue influence on McMillan's work mate.

25.

McMillan sat in his chair behind the desk in his office. He looked at his phone and re-read the message:

F/P's found in vehicle. Nothing to worry about. Nil on weapon. Have located AO. E59JM.

He presumed that *AO. E59JM* was a reference to Albert Oxford and a postcode. He entered the letters and numbers into Google Maps and saw that they related to a church in north east London called St Pauls.

McMillan knew then that he had to pay another flying visit to London to finish the job that his friend Cronk had attempted last summer.

McMillan heard the sound of a moped purring up his driveway. His garage door opened and the figure of Mateo, his accomplice entered the dark space. Limited light was supplied by a table lamp in the windowless room. A computer, printer and photocopier stood in the corner and Mateo, casually leaning against the photocopier asked,

'Any work this week, boss?'

'We might have a little fishing trip next week but I have to return to London to sort out something. In the meantime I need you to dig some dirt on someone to help a lady's divorce. It should be fairly straightforward and the photographic evidence will earn us a fistful of euros.'

The male that Mateo would be looking at worked in the city at an investment company. He was positioned near the top of the chain and was known by his colleagues to be fast and loose with ladies in the employ of the company. He was married to an extremely attractive Senora. They lived together at a large ranch on the outskirts of the city and the senora filled in her time running a stable full of horses which were being trained and educated in the finer points of horse dressage. A vocation that paid well and that allowed the lady to feel she could survive without her husband's money.

Early married life had been passionate but upon discovering that her husband was unable to provide children which she craved for and the fact that she now strongly suspected that her husband was playing the field had led her to telephoning McMillan, whom she had found listed under the heading, 'private investigator.'

Mateo picked up his manilla folder, placed it in the moped pannier and left the McMillan residence.

McMillan booked his flight to the United Kingdom.

26.

Afternoon walks with Helen and with whatever dogs were available were now a regular afternoon occurrence for Albert. He still found that she was shy and reluctant to talk about her life and her previous vocation.

She laughed loudly at the antics of the dogs chasing a ball and Albert was now the beneficiary of a shy smile from the woman when she served the evening repast.

The priest was a busy man, dealing judiciously with his pastoral duties. But he still managed to fit in regular visits to the Plume of Feathers and to the Shoreditch boxing club. His big day was obviously a Sunday when he would take mass at the church, but other days of the week were occupied with visits to those members of his congregation who needed help or comfort.

Interspersed with these duties, Father Michael conducted the occasional christening or funeral service as well as listening attentively to the confessions of his parishioners at the box in the main chapel.

Father Michael Creaney usually seemed to find enough time to visit his other parishioners at the Plume of Feathers.

Albert worked hard in the vegetable garden and the fruits of his labour were now being realised in the form of fresh vegetables served in the kitchen with the evening meal. He also looked forward to his afternoon walks and his evenings were spent between listening to classical music in his room or occasionally accompanying Father Michael on his evening's sojourns, where he had the opportunity to meet up with Nobby and other friends he had made the acquaintance of.

Albert had been taken to the boxing club. A boxing ring dominated the space in the gymnasium but placed round the sides of the gym were various pieces of apparatus associated with the noble art. Bright red leather punch bags shared space with weight lifting benches and barbells.

The priest was obviously a popular figure and was greeted warmly by the instructors and pupils. Father Creaney sat with Albert and watched some of the young prospects go through their paces. The priest also took time-out to talk to the coaches and the young boxers.

Back at the chapel Albert's only 'duty' was to ensure he was available to properly lock down the church at the end of the day. Once the candles had been snuffed, Albert would return the hooded monastic gown to the wardrobe in the foyer and then lock the big front doors after all the lingerers had departed. He was then able to return to his sparse quarters and resume his passion with classical music.

Albert was unaware that he was under surveillance. Whilst toiling in the garden he did not see the figure of a man peering from an adjoining alleyway. Albert broke up compacted earth by using an iron bar with a sharp leading edge which led to a fierce looking point.

This figure also noticed that Albert, on odd occasions, had been assisted by a large man with thick forearms, strong powerful thighs and dressed roughly. He was unshaven and appeared to the onlooker that this man would be a handful if it came to anything physical.

The observer then went to the front of the chapel and entered the church through the main door. He walked up to the pews and sat on a cushioned seat in the back row. The low light in this part of the chapel almost obscured him. He took in the lay-out of the church. A long aisle up the middle of the church led to an altar. The aisle was over-looked by a gallery on either side of the church. The gallery extended to the back of the church but access to this upper area appeared to be out of use and the connecting door to the stairs had been locked.

Sunlight lit the inside of the church and this dim light was augmented by candles contained in candle holders set on plinths.

The man whiled away the time by monitoring his mobile phone which had been placed on 'silent'. He noted customers entering the chapel, making a sign of the cross, and kneeling to pray. Most sat and reflected for some time. When leaving the chapel he noticed that some of them lit a candle in the vestibule before departing the church.

He had sat there for some time and realised that it was getting late. He got up to move but then quickly sat down again when he saw a figure in a monastic gown entering the nave. In his hand he held a long candle snuffer with which he proceeded to extinguish the candles on the plinths down the side of each aisle. The figure also extinguished the lit candles on the altar.

Once this had been completed, the figure proceeded to the church entrance where he was met by the large man who had been assisting him in the garden. This big man then asked those sitting in the vestibule to leave. The observer joined this group and covertly exited the church. He turned around to see the two gardeners lock and bolt the big wooden front doors of the church.

Dennis McMillan had recognised Albert Oxford immediately he had seen him toiling in the garden and now he had seen him dressed in the monastic gown snuffing out candles. The prospect of snuffing out Albert Oxford excited the observer.

The following day, McMillan repeated the process. The weather was inclement and the two gardeners only worked for a short time before collecting some fresh vegetables.

McMillan resumed his vigil in the chapel. At one stage he noticed the priest enter the chapel in his full attire and speak with a young couple. He overheard snippets of conversation that suggested that the young couple were about to embark on a life of matrimony and that they were asking the priest to marry them at a future date.

The couple were shown around the chapel with the priest pointing out where the ceremony would take place and where they were expected to stand.

Once the three of them had left the church, McMillan himself left the church and visited a cafe where he sat for two hours busying himself on his mobile phone and recharging it with permission of the cafe owners.

McMillan returned to the church for the last hour of the day's opening times and resumed his position in the same pew as the previous evening. The closing process was exactly as before save that on this occasion as the temperature had noticeably dropped, Oxford entered the chapel with the hood of the monastic gown over his head. He proceeded to extinguish the lighted candles. Before being asked to leave, McMillan slipped quietly out of the church.

27.

Albert put down the iron bar he was using to break up the compacted ground in the vegetable plot. He left it at the edge of the alleyway. Thomas came across to him and said, 'Albert, your dog's not very well. He looks very sick. You need to have a look at him.'

Albert thanked him and walked across to the dog. He did indeed look poorly. The dog had not eaten the food left for him in a tin bowl but had drunk all the water available in the drinking bowl. Albert refilled the water bowl and left the dog in his kennel. He cleaned up where the dog had been sick and washed it down with the garden hose.

There were no other canine residents at this time. Albert climbed the concrete stairs to his living quarters but first of all knocked quietly on Helen's door. Something he had never done before.

The door opened a fraction and Helen looked out at Albert.

'I'm sorry Helen, but I'm afraid our walk this afternoon will have to be postponed as Bart is not very well.'

'Thank you for telling me Albert,' said Helen, looking concerned.

She quietly closed her door.

Although he was about his dog, Albert felt elation at the fact that this was the first time that Helen had used his name when addressing him.

Albert returned to the dog, who was now asleep.

Later that afternoon Albert returned to check on the dog. Although awake he looked listless and Albert didn't receive the fiercely-wagged tail in recognition. The dog had drunk some more water but had ignored the dog biscuits left for him.

Albert decided to break with protocol and lifted the dog up. Bart was a dead weight in his arms but Albert had taken the decision to take the dog to his room to give him some personal care and attention. He climbed the stairs, unlocked his door and placed the dog on a spare blanket on the floor by the side of his bed. He located a drinking bowl from the kitchen which he took to his room.

At the evening meal Albert sat quietly. Helen served him a plate of soup with bread and asked,

'How is your dog?'

'He's not very well I'm afraid,' replied Albert.

Father Creaney looked concerned but did not say anything. The meal was completed and Albert gathered up the empty plates and took them out to the kitchen area.

'I'm so sorry,' said Helen.

Albert left to return to his room and on passing the priest said 'I will be visiting my parishioners tonight at the Plume.' Albert nodded and went back upstairs to Bart. When Albert entered the room he saw immediately that something was wrong. The dog was still. Albert quickly knelt by the dog and saw that the dog was not breathing. Albert was distraught and yelled out in anguish.

He picked up the dog in the blanket and took it downstairs. He sat with the blanket containing the dog on his lap. The dog was still warm. Albert stroked his face,

'I'm so sorry mate that I couldn't look after you.' Albert buried his face into the dog's neck.

Father Creaney appeared at the end of the alleyway leading onto the garden.

'I hope you haven't had that dog in your room. That looks like one of the blankets from your quarters. I told you dogs are not allowed inside the house.'

'The dog is fucking dead,' screamed Albert at the priest, who recoiled in horror at Albert's language and the news about the dog.

'All I was doing was trying to look after him,' Albert shouted, 'you need to keep your hair on,' Albert yelled.

This obviously stung the priest as he turned quickly on his heel and shouted back to Albert,

'I'll speak with you later.'

'Whatever,' Albert shouted back at the retiring figure.

Albert brought a large canvas bag from his room. He carefully placed the dog contained in the blanket into the canvas bag. He picked up a garden spade and made his way with the canvas bag and spade to the park that had provided him with some of his recent happiest moments with Helen and the dog.

Albert sat on the bench he had often shared with Helen and placed the bag next to him. As the day turned into an evening gloom the park took on a different atmosphere.

Albert sat there for some time and the gloom had turned into darkness only lit by street lamps positioned round the edges of the park.

Albert picked up the bag and spade and walked towards a clump of trees. He picked his spot and started to dig. After thirty minutes of toil he had excavated a rectangular hole.

With a tear trailing down his cheek he said goodbye to his faithful friend. The dog was wrapped in the blanket and carefully placed into the dark brown soil. Albert filled in the hole and replaced the turfs that he had placed to one side.

Albert returned to the bench and thought about a multitude of things. He thought about his existence. His friendship with Father Creaney whom he had just upset. His admiration for the woman who lived in the next room to him but was someone he couldn't or wouldn't approach and get involved with. Now he had lost a dear friend in the dog Bart. Someone he was able to talk to and explain his feelings and problems. Bart had always agreed with him.

Albert sat and watched the city going to sleep in slow motion.

Dennis McMillan sat in the quietest part of the church tucked well away out of sight and in virtual darkness. He sat and waited. On the wooden floor he had placed the iron bar from the alleyway. The one that Oxford had used for gardening.

He looked at his watch and saw that it was fast approaching the time that Oxford would enter the church to turn out the lights. But first he had to be careful that he wasn't spotted by the big bruiser who usually emptied the church of those praying and sitting quietly. He slid down below the height of the pew.

Father Michael Creaney had drained the last of the Guinness in his glass. He made his farewells.

'I'll see you all on Sunday at mass,' he shouted jokingly.

He exited onto the street to the sounds of laughter coming from the pub punters who obviously appreciated his futile attempt at humour.

The priest did not expect to see any of them at mass.

The evening had turned cool and he turned up the collar of his coat as he made his way back to the church.

On his way back he reflected on the difference of opinion he had had with Albert. As far as he was concerned the matter was finished and he hoped the spat would not affect his relationship with him.

Thomas had a cursory glance around the nave of the church but didn't see the figure of McMillan hunched below the pew at the back of the church.

Thomas knew that Albert would be appearing soon to snuff out the lit candles. He asked those in the front porch of the church to leave, telling them that the premises were closed for the day and would be open again for business as usual the following morning.

Albert made his way slowly back to the church. He had decided that he should apologise to the priest but deliberated as to whether he would make those apologies that evening or the following morning.

Father Creaney approached his church. He could see through the open doors of the church that the candles in the foyer and deeper inside the church were still alight. He was disappointed that his altercation with Albert seemed to have affected their working relationship and friendship.

Dennis McMillan raised himself from his uncomfortable position. With his gloved hand he gripped the iron bar and lay in wait.

A hooded monastic figure entered the nave of the church, armed with a candle snuffer. The figure walked up the left hand aisle which was furthest away from McMillan. He carefully extinguished the lit candles on his route.

At the top of the church, just before the altar, the figure made the sign of the cross. McMillan hadn't seen Oxford do this before. The hooded figure then commenced walking down the other aisle in the direction of McMillan.

As he snuffed out the last candle in the main body of the church he walked past McMillan who was lurking in the now darkened shadows. Once the figure had cleared McMillan, McMillan stepped out of the pew behind him.

Raising the iron bar, he brought it down with a crushing blow on the back of the figure's skull. The victim fell onto the marbled floor. McMillan aimed two more blows to the back of the man's head. Blood seeped through the hood.

Convinced that Oxford was now dead, McMillan dropped the weapon next to the bloodied figure and slowly made his way out through the foyer.

It was now deserted. McMillan carefully pulled the big doors closed but they remained unlocked. McMillan walked quietly away into the darkness.

Albert turned the corner and approached the church. He

saw that the big doors were closed. He presumed that the priest had closed up the church. Something else he would have to apologise for in the morning.

Albert saw that although the doors were closed, they had not been locked. He pulled open one of the doors and entered the foyer.

He could see that the candles had been extinguished and presumed that either the priest or Thomas had performed the task.

He left the church pulling the big doors closed. He locked the door using the spare key he had been given by Father Creaney.

Albert retired to his room and lay on his bed reflecting on the events of the day. Sad and disappointed about his dog Bart, and also sad about the way he had handled himself with Father Creaney. He would apologise to him in the morning.

28.

The next morning Albert went down to breakfast. Helen placed some toast on the table and Albert helped himself to some cereal. He noticed that the priest was not present.

Once he had finished breakfast, Albert used the alleyway to gain access to the garden. He saw that the big doors of the chapel were still closed. He presumed that the priest was inside the church on work-related business and he wanted to take the opportunity to speak to him and apologise for the verbal spat that had occurred yesterday. He was alarmed however, to see that the doors were still padlocked.

He opened the doors and saw that the candles in the main part of the church had not been lit. This was a task always performed by Father Creaney first thing in the morning before he saw to the homeless gathering on the front steps of the church.

Even though the candles had not been lit, there was enough ambient light through the high stained glass windows to see inside the church.

Albert peered towards the altar but couldn't see the priest. He listened outside the confessional box but heard nothing. He was about to exit the church when he noticed a crumpled figure lying on the marble floor in the aisle on the other side of the pews. Albert saw that the prostate figure was lying face down and was wearing the monastic gown that Albert sometimes wore when performing candle-snuffing duties.

The figure appeared lifeless and Albert feared the worst. Albert saw that a pool of blood surrounded the hood and this pool had solidified. Albert's worst fears were confirmed when he noticed that under the hood there appeared to be a displaced toupee which was matted in blood. Albert felt for a pulse on the figure's neck but quickly realised that the body was, indeed, lifeless.

Albert rushed to the kitchen, picked up the phone and dialled 999. He asked for the police and on being connected said, in a calm voice,

'I've just found the body of a dead man inside the church of St Pauls.' Albert supplied the address.

Helen's face paled and she started sobbing quietly. Albert sat her down.

Thomas came through the door for his morning cup of tea and Albert told him the news of his discovery. Thomas looked shocked and sat next to Helen.

After some five minutes, Albert could hear the sounds of police sirens. He went outside to greet the police officers. He spoke to the more senior of the two uniformed officers and led the two of them to the door of the church. He pointed out the lifeless body. The senior constable checked for a pulse and came back to the door of the church where Albert was standing.

The constable spoke to his colleague who went to the marked police car and from the boot took out a substantial roll of 'police incident' tape. The two officers sealed off the front of the church. Whilst this was happening, an unmarked police car arrived at the church. The driver of the car was a young fresh-faced man wearing round framed spectacles which looked too big for his young pale face. He was wearing a light brown two-piece suit over his thin frame and his pale green shirt and floral tie completed the garb of the young modern-day detective. He was carrying a clip-board.

Stepping out from the front passenger side of the car was an older, bulkier man. His bulbous strawberry nose, planted on a bloated face, gave indication of his propensity to take aboard copious amounts of alcohol.

He spoke to the two uniformed officers, who by now, had been joined by several other officers. The senior detective entered the church and reappeared soon after. He instructed the junior detective, known in police circles as his bag carrier, to summon a full forensic team to fully audit the scene of what he suspected was murder most foul.

Albert, Helen and Thomas were pointed out to the senior detective. All four retired to the kitchen. Helen had stopped crying but dabbed at her eyes occasionally with a white linen handkerchief. Thomas's face was completely expressionless.

'My name's Detective Superintendent Carpenter,' the detective said. 'I am attached to the Area Major Investigation Pool and I'd welcome your cooperation in this matter.'

'Young Coleman, who is outside at the moment, is my

assistant and he will speak with you all shortly. In the meantime I'd ask you all to remain here until he has spoken to you.'

Albert, Helen and Thomas remained in the kitchen. Helen made a pot of tea but the conversation was minimal. Albert stared at the floor and tried to comprehend what had happened. Who would want to bludgeon to death a harmless, gentle man trying his best to do a bit of good in the world. He would be a huge loss to the community.

Coleman had utilised the uniform police officers to seal off the road outside the church and the police tape had been extended to keep sightseers well away from the front door of the church.

A camera crew had arrived and was attempting to film from a distance. A smartly dressed man was speaking into the camera lens whilst a scruffy individual held an extended fluffy microphone under his chin.

A national newspaper reporter had arrived with dicta-phone and a mobile and he was shortly joined by two local newspaper reporters. They compared notes.

For the three people in the kitchen, the day progressed slowly. During the afternoon, Carpenter and Coleman appeared and took them individually into the Father's living area. They all gave an account of their movements the previous day. Albert told them of the burial of his dog but did not not mention the heated exchange of words with the priest.

Once this had been completed, all three were told that they were free to resume doing what they wanted but that the scene of the crime was out of bounds. Helen told

Albert that she was in no mood to prepare any food and that it was her intention to retire to her room to pray. Thomas left to return to his room in the hostel provided by a homeless charity.

Albert pondered what to do. He felt he owed it to Michael Creaney's personal friends at the Plume of Feathers to tell them personally.

At the public house the news had been received with much anguish and anger. The wave of emotion suggested that if the assembled crowd could get their hands on the perpetrator the likelihood of a mob-lynching was definitely in the realms of possibility.

Albert did not stay long at the public house but returned to his quarters at the church. He also felt an anger that reminded him of his feelings when he and his neighbours fought back against criminality in their neighbourhood. That had been a scary adventure but Albert was determined that he would seek the ultimate revenge on whoever had killed his friend.

The night was still. No barking dogs from the kennels below. But still Albert couldn't sleep. He would have loved to have heard his Jack Russell barking. He tossed and turned and the early light pervading through his thin curtains was a welcome release from his torment. But not for long!

29.

Detective Superintendent Bryan Carpenter and Detective Sergeant John Coleman sat in Carpenter's small office which was situated along the corridor from the main incident room which was the central hub of the enquiry. They both nursed a mug of tea and discussed the events of the previous day.

'So, where are we with this?' asked Carpenter, sipping at his mug.

'Three statements from neighbours which are quite revealing,' replied Coleman. 'Plus we have an iron bar, possibly the weapon used, which is undergoing urgent forensic examination. Background checks are underway looking at Oxford, Thomas Cannon, the victim and the ex-nun, Helen, who lived on the premises.'

'Oxford lived on the premises as well didn't he? Are Oxford and the ex-nun an item?' asked Carpenter. 'She is a strikingly attractive woman.'

'No they don't appear to be. They have separate rooms.'

'Okay what have we got on this character Oxford? He seems like a person of interest.'

'A person of interest for sure,' replied Coleman. 'He

played a major part in that gang of vigilantes who decided they were going to take the law into their own hands and sort out the criminal gangs in their area of east London. They were directly responsible for the deaths or disappearance of four people, but also indirectly involved in the deaths of another six. He fled to Spain.'

'What happened to him then?' asked Carpenter.

'A Detective Inspector traced him to Spain, but then compromised himself by allowing himself to be tape-recorded. The upshot was that this Detective Inspector Marker and his Detective Constable John McEvoy were exposed as being corrupt and subsequently managed to kill themselves at an underground station in central London in a bizarre incident which just happened to be witnessed by Oxford.'

'Yes, I remember that now, and as a result of Marker's corruption, quite a few prisoners were released from their sentences early as it was thought that their convictions were unsafe. I also recall that most of his enquiries he was conducting at the time were shelved.'

'Yes sir, that's correct. The case against Oxford was dropped and he returned to Spain. However, it didn't end there. You'll remember William Cronk from the north London area major investigation pool. He was in the last throes of his life, suffering from terminal cancer related issues. He took it upon himself to visit Spain and shot Oxford in the head. He then took his own life, but, miraculously, Oxford survived and finished up with a metal plate in his head. That metal plate becomes significant as, some weeks ago, an attempt was made on Albert Oxford's life and he survived the shooting as the bullet hit the metal plate.'

'One lucky man,' said Carpenter.

'He is indeed, sir. He decided that living in that canal boat was not good for his health and it was then that he found himself living at the church. He does odd jobs round the chapel and tends to the garden and the stray dogs. He turns his hand to fixing problems with plumbing and electrics and keeps himself to himself, apparently.'

'Okay, so what have we got on this Thomas Cannon?'

'From what I've been able to piece together Cannon is a homeless ex veteran. Although officially classified as homeless he has a room in a men's hostel in Stoke Newington. He helps out at the chapel. Not a lot of work but he gets rewarded with a meal or a sandwich. He suffers mentally but that can be traced back to his time serving with the armed forces in Afghanistan. I'm sure that he was probably part of an SAS team.'

'And the ex-nun?' asked Carpenter.

'That's exactly what she is,' replied Coleman, 'a nun who was working out of the big convent in Finchley. She is Irish and was placed to work in London. It would appear that she came off the rails slightly. Nothing serious, but felt so embarrassed about it that she felt she had to leave. Father Creaney, the victim in this case, heard about her slip-up and offered her the opportunity to be housekeeper and cook at St Paul's church in exchange for accommodation.'

'Excellent so far,' said Carpenter, 'and what can you tell me about the victim?'

'If I was religious he would've been the perfect priest for me. Kind, caring, considerate and very popular with his flock. He enjoyed a drink, Guinness in particular, and appeared to be a really nice bloke.'

'Thank you John. I've just read through most of the statements taken from the location of the crime. Very interesting. I think we should invite Oxford down here to have a chat with us in the interview room.'

'Okay, Boss.'

Later that afternoon, Albert was sitting in the kitchen drinking a cup of tea prepared for him by Helen. She had been very quiet. Quieter than usual, and her red-rimmed eyes betrayed the fact that she had been crying. There was no conversation between the two when Albert suddenly heard a knock at the outside door.

Albert went to answer the door and saw Detective Sergeant Coleman accompanied by another officer in plain clothes and two young uniformed officers.

'Albert Oxford, I am arresting you for the murder of Father Michael Creaney. You do not have to say anything. But it may harm your defence if you do not mention when questioned something which you later rely on in court. Anything you do say may be given in evidence. Do you understand?'

Albert was taken aback. He glanced at Helen who turned her eyes to the floor and started to cry.

'I understand the caution, but I do not understand why you have arrested me,' replied Albert.

One of the uniformed officers placed a pair of handcuffs on Albert's wrists. He was led out to a marked police car and placed in the back seat. The uniformed officer sat next to him. The other uniformed officer took up his position behind the wheel of the car and drove the three of them to the police station at Whitechapel.

Albert was taken to the custody suite at the police station. The cuffs were removed. John Coleman appeared and informed the custody sergeant that Albert Oxford had been arrested for murder.

Albert was searched and his belongings placed in a plastic property bag. He consented to having his fingerprints taken and a sample of his DNA was also taken.

'Do you understand why you're here?' the Custody Suite sergeant asked Albert.

'I've been informed, but it's nothing to do with me,' replied Albert.

Albert was handed a grey tracksuit and was asked to deposit his own clothing into an exhibit bag. He was taken to the cell block and taken to a cell with the door already open. He was ushered inside.

Albert sat on the solitary wooden chair in the room and took stock of his surroundings. A concrete bench had a rubber mattress lying on top of it. Folded neatly on top of the mattress was a flimsy acrylic blanket. At the foot of the bed, and furthest from the cell door, was a basic stainless steel toilet without a seat. A small sink made up the rest of the furnishings. The light was provided by a single bulb set in the ceiling and protected by a wire mesh. There was no window and when the door was shut it clanged loudly. In the door was a small rectangular metal aperture. The metal flap had been closed from the outside.

Albert decided that because there was nothing else to do, the best course of action was to lay out on the uncomfortable mattress and try to get some sleep.

30.

News of the murder had spread. Nobby, who had been responsible for introducing Albert to the priest, went to the church. He noticed that Thomas Cannon was hanging around by the church door which still had prohibitive police tape across the entrance to the church itself.

'What a dreadful state of affairs,' said Nobby'

It gets worse, Nobby. Albert has been arrested for the murder of Father Michael.'

Nobby was visibly shocked.

'That's ridiculous,' he replied, 'there's no way that Albert would have done anything like that. I know he's had a dodgy past but he and Michael were the best of mates.'

'I agree Nobby. I don't envy you the job of telling all his mates down at the Plume of Feathers.'

'What's happened to the nun?' asked Nobby.

'Ex nun to be exact. She didn't want to go home to Ireland out of embarrassment but I think she's made the decision to return to her part of Ireland and try to make things up with her mother. From what the Father told me I don't think her mother is very well.'

'Bloody hell. It must have been something serious for

her not to go back home in the first place. Do you know what she did wrong? Not that it's any of my business.'

'Apparently it was nothing of any importance but she is a very conscientious lady and felt as if she had let herself, her family, the faith and God, down. She had feelings for a man. That was all, nothing else, nothing happened but she couldn't handle it and when she reported it to Mother Superior, there was no going back or changing her mind.'

'What a shame for her, I know she had a lot of time for the Father.'

'What will you tell them at the pub Nobby?'

'I'll tell it as it is. In fact I'm going to make my way down there now. Keep in touch Thomas.'

Nobby wrote down his mobile number on a scrap of paper which he pressed into the giant man's big fist.

31.

The metal wicker gate on Albert's cell door slid open. A pair of eyes peered into the cell.

'You'll be taken up for an interview shortly, but in the meantime I've brought you a drink and something to eat.'

A polystyrene beaker of tea was placed on the ledge of the aperture. This was gratefully accepted by Albert and in its place was deposited a white-bread cheese sandwich wrapped in cling film.

Albert picked up the sandwich and thought it once might have been at its freshest five or six days ago. Nevermind, it was something to get his teeth stuck into, hopefully, not literally.

Ten minutes later a rattling of keys was followed by the opening of the cell door. A middle-aged detective beckoned Albert to follow him. Albert dutifully trailed after him and was led into a sparsely furnished room, in the middle of which was a plain wooden table with four wooden chairs, two on one side facing the other two.

Seated at one of the seats was Detective Sergeant Coleman. Albert was invited to sit in a chair opposite Coleman. Between them on the table was a recording device. The detective who had brought Albert from the cell sat next to Coleman. Coleman switched on the recording device.

'Albert Oxford, I am here to interview you about the murder of Father Michael Creaney.' Coleman then repeated the police caution which he had administered when arresting Albert.

'This interview is being recorded on this device,' pointing at the tape recorder, 'and the interview's also being recorded on film.' Coleman at this point indicated a wall-mounted camera on a wall with the lens facing Albert.

'You are entitled to have a solicitor present during this interview. Is there anyone you would wish to be here to represent you?'

'I don't have a solicitor,' replied Albert. The only solicitor that he had dealings with was a man called Bernie who he used to have a drink with in the Black Lion pub in Plaistow. They shared a love of the same football team. But Bernie would be retired now and probably spending his days on the golf course.

'There is a duty solicitor on hand who can sit with you and advise you. Do you wish to take up his services?'

'It'd be better than nothing,' answered Albert.

The other officer left the room and ten minutes later returned accompanied by the duty solicitor.

Albert weighed him up. Fifty years old, overweight, a couple of strands of hair brushed over a balding head in a ridiculous comb-over. He wore a crumpled brown suit that looked slept-in. The same colour waistcoat had a food stain down the front. His rimmed glasses perched on the end of a bulbous nose that had seen days of hard drinking. Albert could smell the alcohol from five feet away.

'This is Mr Perkins, the duty solicitor,' said Detective Sergeant Coleman.

'Well, I guessed it wasn't Rumpole of the Bailey,' replied Albert.

Perkins seemed to take exception to this and curtly said to Albert,

'If you don't require my services then I have better things to do.'

Albert thought of a drying-out clinic or even a bath but replied,

'No, it's okay, you can sit in and listen.'

'For the purposes of this interview I want to state that I have not had the opportunity to speak to my client about these matters, so I will be advising him to say nothing in response to any of your questions,' Perkins said.

Albert was impressed and surprised by this statement. Maybe he was distantly related to Rumpole.

'I take note of your objections Mr Perkins,' said Coleman, 'but I still wish to put some questions to Mr Oxford. Whether he answers them or not is up to him, but I have cautioned him and told him of the opportunity to tell me his version of events.'

'Mr Oxford, where were you between the hours of 9pm and 12 midnight on the day that Father Michael Creaney was murdered?'

Albert went to answer but caught a look from the solicitor Perkins and said,

'No comment'.

'You told me earlier that you were burying your dog in a park in Stoke Newington. Is that correct?'

'No comment.'

'Can you explain to me how your fingerprints were found on the iron bar that was used to kill Michael Creaney?'

'No comment.'

'The deceased's blood was found on the sleeve of your pullover. Could you please tell me how that got there?'

'No comment.'

'Earlier that evening, two witnesses claim that you and Father Creaney had a loud heated exchange of words. Can you tell me what your argument was about?'

'No comment.'

'Mr Oxford in light of your refusal to answer questions I will terminate this interview now. You may want to have a discussion with your solicitor in private and afterwards you will be returned to your cell and after I have had the opportunity to speak to my boss and the Crown Prosecution Service you will almost certainly be formally charged with the murder of Michael Creaney.'

Coleman switched off the recording device and left the interview room with his fellow officer.

Perkins looked at Albert and placed a finger to his lips. He said quietly to Albert,

'Is there anything you want to ask me, now?'

'Yes, what happens now?

'It would seem that they think they have enough evidence to charge you with murder and once that formality has taken place you will appear before a magistrate who will remand you until a trial date or plea entry hearing can be arranged. I will instruct a barrister to represent you on a legal aid basis. The probability is you will be remanded in custody but the barrister will be at court to represent you on that matter.'

32.

Two hours later Albert Oxford was formally charged with the murder of Michael Creaney. This took place in the custody suite. Albert was placed back in his cell.

Although he knew he had nothing to do with the murder of his friend he felt some anxiety about possible miscarriages of justice. And, more importantly, who had killed the priest?

He did not sleep and was constantly prevented from doing so by the wild shouting of drunk and disorderly prisoners in adjoining cells.

When dawn broke Albert washed and partook of a supplied sandwich and a polystyrene cup of tea. He was collected from his cell, handcuffed and taken out into the police yard where he was placed into a white prison van. The van contained individual cubicles and Albert sat down in this tight confined space. A small barred window allowed him to monitor his progress in the van towards the magistrate's court.

When the van arrived at the Magistrates Court, Albert was removed from his confined space and taken by a burly prison officer into the cells below the court.

His handcuffs were removed. A fresh-faced young man appeared at his doorway. The cell door was opened by a guard and the immaculately dressed young man said,

'Mr Albert Oxford, my name is Anthony Mellish. I have been asked to represent you at your court hearing today. The office of your solicitor Mr Perkins, has asked me to look after your interests. There will not be any point in applying for bail today as the prosecution solicitors will quote your likelihood to abscond, as you have a history of living in Spain.'

'How long will I be in custody?' asked Albert.

'It will depend on what happens when the case comes before the trial judge. Depending on your plea or conviction the amount of time you spend in custody could be quite substantial.'

'What happens now?'

'After this hearing you will be remanded in custody to await proceedings at a trial court. You'll almost certainly be remanded to Her Majesty's Prison at Belmarsh.'

Albert stepped into the dock of the Magistrates Court. He looked round. In front of him on the Magistrate's Bench sat three people, one of whom was a woman who looked down her nose at him as if he was something she had picked up on her shoes. Albert stared back at her. The two male magistrates didn't bother looking at him.

Albert looked round the court. Three reporters fought for a bit of space on the small bench and table provided for the sole local newspaper reporter.

Albert turned round to the small public gallery and was pleased to spot Nobby's dark face. Nobby gave a thumbs-up sign. This pleased Albert as he had been unsure of what the reaction would have been from his close friends and the others at the Plume of Feathers.

Albert was asked by the clerk of the court to confirm his name and the charge of murder was put to him.

Albert pleaded '*not guilty*'. Albert's barrister confirmed to the bench that no bail application would be made on this occasion. Albert was duly remanded in custody by the female magistrate to appear before a Crown Court at a date yet to be fixed.

After a short wait in the court cells Albert was taken out by a prison warder and placed into the white prison van. Albert looked out the window of the van. As the van exited the courtyard of the Magistrates Court Albert saw a crowd of people shouting and gesticulating at the van.

Albert mused that something had obviously upset them and then, in horror, realised that he was the subject of their opprobrium. A couple of cameras flashed at his window.

The journey in the van was uncomfortable. The heat in the cell cubicles was almost unbearable and the lack of suspension on the vehicle meant that Albert was jolted and thrown about on every turn and speed bump.

Albert could see out of the window that the van was now approaching what appeared to be a high security prison. Tall brick walls were topped with rolls of barbed wire and security cameras were placed in abundance along the perimeter wall.

The van pulled into an inner security space. The gates behind the van were closed before the van advanced through another layer of fence security.

When the van stopped the occupants of the van were removed from the van cells and a line of six prisoners were led into a security area within the body of the prison.

Albert was duly processed. This included a full strip search and after completion Albert was handed the uni-formed garb of a high security prisoner. Donning his grey tracksuit and hi-viz orange vest, Albert was taken to the cell area of the prison.

The first thing that struck Albert was the cacophony of noise with inmates shouting across landings. Some of this was light-hearted and some was menacing. The next thing that struck him was the inordinate amount of metal and steel which made up the wing of this prison. He was taken up a metal staircase to a landing. Albert avoided eye contact and was taken to a cell door. The elderly prison officer said,

'This is your new home Mr Oxford. Your roommate is a prisoner called Edward. You won't have any problem with him. Keep yourself to yourself. Avoid the nutters. You will soon spot who they are. Good luck.'

Albert stepped inside the cell door and it clanged shut behind him. A stainless steel toilet was tucked behind a toughened plastic modesty screen. A small sink with a single tap stood next to the toilet. A small barred window with toughened glass sat high on the wall. Light was provided by a bulb embedded into the high ceiling. The floor was bare concrete and on one wall was placed a wooden table and one solitary wooden chair. A television set with a flickering silent picture sat on the table. A wire serving as an antennae stretched upwards towards the light of the window and was held in place by a hardened piece of chewing gum.

Down the side of the other wall stretched a double bunk bed. The bottom bed was occupied by a large man who was liberally decorated with tattoos showing allegiance to various women and a football team. He had a shaved head and a large paunch and wore the obligatory uniform of grey tracksuit. He gave the appearance of having just awoken and stared at Albert.

Albert nodded at him and got a nod in return.

'Top bunk's yours but only because I can't get up there. No snoring or you'll get a slap.'

There was just the merest trace of a smile when he said this.

'I don't snore,' said Albert.

'I'll be the judge of that. My wash bag is on the right hand side of the sink. Don't touch it or you'll get a slap. You'll get a visit later and be handed your own washing gear. What are you in here for?'

'They have accused me of murder but I didn't do it.'

Albert's cellmate burst out laughing.

'You and 1200 others in here. Nobody is guilty. Strange that, don't you think?'

Albert remained silent.

The big man said,

'I'm Edward, but you can call me Ted if you wish.'

'What are you in here for, Ted,' asked Albert.

'I rob banks. Not with a shotgun, you understand, but by scamming them. It's more of a technical crime and I really shouldn't be in here.'

Albert smiled and received a wide smile back from Ted.

Albert swung himself up onto the top bunk and lay flat with his hands behind his head on the basic pillow.

His immediate future existence was now set out, only to be interrupted by feeding, washing, controlled exercise walks, watching Ted's choice of television programmes and the boredom of confinement.

33.

Mateo was riding his small motorcycle towards the villa where his boss Dennis McMillan lived. He was going to report to him the latest developments on the divorce he had been tasked to investigate for McMillan.

As he neared the driveway he turned a corner but found that the road had been blocked by an old flat truck. Two middle-aged men stood in the middle of the road and beckoned him to slow down and stop.

Mateo felt uneasy but did as he was requested. Mateo pulled the bike back on to its stand. The two men approached him. Mateo had not seen them before but guessed that they belonged to either of the gangs bossed by El Caballo or El Poderoso. He hoped that they belonged to Caballo's gang as the reputation of the Poderosians was fearsome.

One of the men took hold of Mateo's elbow and steered him towards the truck. He was placed in the middle of the leather bench seat in the front of the cab section of the truck between the two men.

The senior of the men did all the talking. He informed Mateo that his life was in danger if he did not do their bidding. He was told that the gang knew of his activities with McMillan in their criminal enterprise securing grade A drugs from a north African firm of smugglers. Mateo remained silent.

Mateo was told quite specifically what would happen to him and his family if he refused to accede to their demands. It included the removal of body parts. Body parts that were quite personal to Mateo. He had to cut off all contact with McMillan and had to take himself away from his home where he lived with his sister and mother.

The younger man relieved Mateo of his mobile phone and removed the sim card. The mobile phone was returned to Mateo. He was handed a burner mobile phone which he was told was a means of contact between himself and the gang.

He was informed that he was not the target but that the spotlight was firmly fixed on McMillan. As a reward for his compliance he was informed that his job as a drugs courier would be resumed once McMillan had been dealt with.

Mateo was worried. He feared this gang but also feared the repercussions from McMillan who he knew had a nasty temper which he had exhibited in the past.

Mateo's first task was to remove himself from his family home. After informing his sister that he had to disappear for a few weeks he packed a canvas bag with some clothes and toiletries and made plans to jump on a bus to visit a friend some 80 kilometres away to the north of where he lived.

McMillan sat in his garage-cum-office fuming at the lateness of Mateo who had failed to appear at the time they had arranged to meet. McMillan rang Mateo's mobile phone but was informed that the phone was unreachable.

McMillan's phone suddenly buzzed with a text message: *Clown. Have you seen the news?*

McMillan switched on his computer and trawled through various news sites relating to the UK. His mouth dropped open when he read about an Irish Catholic priest being murdered in his church in north London. Another report said that a man called Albert Oxford had been arrested and was currently on remand in a south east London prison awaiting trial for the murder of the priest.

McMillan carefully closed down the computer. He picked it up and threw it against the far wall of his garage.

He realised he couldn't take a chance on returning to the UK just in case there was any evidence leading to his involvement in the murder.

34.

McMillan decided that he would have a drive to the village of Tajeda. Mateo lived here with his mother and sister. McMillan intended to find out what Mateo was up to and was angry that Mateo had not been in touch, but he had to be careful. The hoodlum, El Caballo, who he had already crossed swords with, lived on the outer fringes of the village in his palatial villa.

The village was nestled in the low foothills some 30 kilometres from the coast and was a pretty village with nearly every house whitewashed making the whole vista stand out in the frequent and plentiful sunshine.

Many of the small houses had small gardens which were tended to with care by the occupants. Freshly washed clothes hung in the small breeze. The pavements and roads were clean and free of weeds and rubbish.

As McMillan looked down on the scene he felt a small pang of envy of a seemingly idyllic life-style but almost as quickly dismissed those thoughts. Without a supply of ill-gotten cash McMillan would be unable to lead the lifestyle he had come to enjoy. His secret trysts with Camella were right at the top of his list.

He parked his car and walked down the narrow street where Mateo lived. He knocked on the brown wooden door. After a short wait the door opened and McMillan was greeted by the wizened face of an elderly woman who he took to be Mateo's mother.

He spoke Spanish and asked her the whereabouts of Mateo. She scowled at McMillan and told him abruptly that Mateo had gone away for a few weeks and would not be returning at any time in the near future.

It was McMillan's turn to scowl and he turned smartly on his heel. He walked away and returned to his car.

McMillan pondered his next move. The drug overlord who he obtained the packages for lived in a village some 25 kilometres north in a small town called Passina. McMillan knew that he wouldn't be able to gain personal access to El Poderoso but McMillan felt he had to get a message to him personally.

McMillan drove to Passina. There could not have been a more stark contrast than with the village he had just left. The former was a picturesque, thriving village whereas Passina was dark, uninviting and possessed a menacing feel. The village sat at the foot of a mountain which did not allow unfettered sunshine to the buildings. These buildings were dark and foreboding. The town consisted mainly of a large square with houses built onto the edges of the square. The buildings had extended outwards over the years.

El Poderoso lived in a large four-storey apartment block which overlooked the square. There were no happy vibes emanating from this place. El Poderosa ruled with an iron fist and the villagers were fearful of him, his henchmen and especially his vicious temper and nasty streak. The young men of the village moved away from the village as soon as circumstances allowed. This left an increasingly ageing populus who stayed in situ and did their collective best not to poke the 'big dog'.

McMillan parked his car and walked along a street which led onto the square. He approached El Poderoso's street door. A tall thin man clad in denim slouched by the entrance.

McMillan told the guard that he wanted to get a message to his boss and that was to inform him that his partner Mateo had disappeared and the smuggling operation would have to be put on hold for a short time.

The door-keeper told him to wait. McMillan scowled. He wasn't used to being ordered about. But he didn't have much choice. Five minutes later the man re-appeared and invited McMillan into the house. He was led down a long corridor and then up to flights of marble stair-casing. At the top of the stairs the guard took McMillan to a large oak-panelled door. He knocked and McMillan was ushered inside into the office of El Poderoso.

McMillan acknowledged El Poderoso with a curt nod. The crime boss stared at McMillan. He was surprised to see that El Podereoso was wearing a light blue fine-wool scarf despite the temperature in the room.

McMillan was not invited to sit down. He explained to the crime boss that because of the temporary absence of his assistant Mateo, he would be unable to provide the regular supply of narcotics to the cartel.

El Poderoso did not reply immediately but seemed to be

considering his reply carefully. Eventually he informed McMillan that if he could not supply the drugs then El Poderoso himself would appoint someone to take his place.

McMillan was shocked, but sensibly did not argue his case. He was dismissed with a flick of the hand. McMillan returned to his car. He sat for a while mulling things over. He reluctantly realised that he had messed up and his ploy hadn't worked out as planned.

If he was to miss out on the collection and delivery it would seriously impact his lifestyle and bank account. Only two people on the Spanish side knew of the collection arrangements. One of them, Mateo, had disappeared, and it slowly dawned on McMillan that he was being frozen out of the operation. He sat plotting what form his revenge would take.

In a village some 40 kilometres away, Mateo received a call on his new burner mobile phone. He was told that he was now the person responsible for the collection of the contraband. He was instructed to purchase a small motorboat and to moor it at a marina 30 kilometres south of where McMillan had moored his own craft. Mateo was told that once this was all in place he would receive instructions as to the time and coordinates of the next package to arrive from North Africa.

35.

The boredom of the routine in Belmarsh Prison was repetitive. Sleep was difficult due to the nocturnal noises of a prison, his cellmate's toilet routines and the close confinement.

Mealtimes were an opportunity for Albert to leave the cell but Edward had warned him to avoid making eye contact, especially with the jihadists and the African nutters. Edward had a way with words, thought Albert.

The relentless monotony was broken by a prison officer who informed Albert that he had a visitor but that it would take place in the appointed secure area for visitors. Albert donned his hi-viz slipover and was led to the secure area for visits.

Once inside the small room Albert saw that on his side of the strengthened glass partition was a plastic chair. He saw a microphone and looked upwards and saw that the room was covered by a camera. On the other side of the glass partition sat Nobby.

Nobby smiled at Albert. Albert felt a huge sense of relief. He had wondered how his arrest had been received by his friends but Nobby's smile went some way to reassure him that the situation was better than he feared.

'Thanks for coming, Nobby. I can't believe what has happened. How are things?'

'Albert, there isn't a single person who believes that you're guilty. The mood down at the Plume is anger mainly and there have been strong words. We're all on your side, Albert. Is there anything I can do for you? Do you need anything?'

'Not really, Nobby, but thank you. What's happened to Thomas and the nun, Helen?'

'Thomas sits outside the church all day. The church is looking to replace Michael but the place is still closed up. Nobody has seen Helen and Thomas thinks she may have gone back to Ireland.'

'Did she say anything before she left, Nobby?'

'No, not a thing.'

Albert talked about the regime in prison and said that he hoped that the court appearance would come up fairly quickly.

At the end of the allotted time, Nobby was invited to leave the room and a prison officer escorted Albert back to his cell.

He lay thinking about the visit. He was pleased that he seemed to have the support of his friends but was upset that he hadn't had the chance to speak to Helen and convince her of his innocence.

He fell asleep on his mattress and slept fitfully for the first time in many days. The fact that his friends believed him had obviously helped him.

36.

etective Sergeant Ted Fuller sat at his office desk with a cup of decaffeinated coffee. He had a problem to contemplate. He had spent most of the morning on the telephone obtaining flight manifestos of airlines which flew in and out of Stansted airport at the time of the attempted killing of Albert Oxford.

Once he had learned of the arrest of Oxford for the murder of the Irish priest he expanded his search to enquire of manifestos relating to the time of the priest's murder.

Armed with the information, he sought an appointment with his superior officer Detective Superintendent Williams at Divisional headquarters later that afternoon.

Williams invited Ted Fuller to sit in a chair facing him and was separated by a large oak desk. From a drawer on his side of the table Williams produced a bottle of malt whisky and two crystal cut glasses. He poured a liberal measure into each glass.

'It's not very often I get a personal visit from you Ted, so this must be fairly important.'

'I think it is sir and I'd like to lay out a case before you and see what you think.'

'Go on Ted,' said Williams.

'You will recall sir that I am investigating the attempted murder of a man called Albert Oxford.'

'I have been following that case, Ted,' said Williams, taking a sip of his scotch.

'I have identified a possible suspect for the shooting. His name is Dennis McMillan. He is an ex-police officer, now working as a private detective in Spain. He left the police force under a bit of a cloud. He was a good friend of the late Bill Cronk who committed suicide after an attempt on Oxford's life in Spain. Oxford survived that attempt and had a metal plate inserted in his left temple. Oxford also survived another attempt on his life. Someone shot him on his canal boat but miraculously the sniper's bullet hit the same piece of metal.'

Both men took a sip of their whisky and Ted Fuller continued.

'I recovered footage of a car I believe to be the assailant's from CCTV footage at Hackney Marshes car park. The car is registered to Bill Cronk. I circulated details of this car and it was found in a multi-storey car park in Stratford. A fingerprint in the car belongs to this Dennis McMillan. A short distance away from the car we found parts of a rifle. I believe that this was the rifle used to shoot Oxford. Unfortunately this weapon came back clean, forensically.'

Ted Fuller paused and took a sip from his glass. Williams topped up the glasses with another measure of the malt amber liquid.

'I have checked the flight manifesto of airlines before

and after the attempt on Oxford's life and it reveals that Dennis McMillan flew into the UK a few days before the assassination attempt and left the UK later the same day of the attempt.

'I submitted a report to the Crown Prosecution Service with all the details but they informed me that there wasn't enough evidence to justify a trip to Spain to interview McMillan.'

'Yes, I was made aware of that Ted, but where are we now? I have a feeling that you are going to develop this story.'

'Indeed, sir.' Another sip of whisky followed.

'Albert Oxford was a resident on his canal boat on the River Lea Navigation Canal at the time of the latest attempt on his life. Because of the attempt on his life he had to move away from the canal boat. He was offered, and accepted, accommodation with a Catholic priest, Father Michael Creaney.'

Williams emitted an audible gasp.

'The priest who has just been murdered?' asked Williams.

'The very same,' said Fuller, 'and Albert Oxford has been charged with his murder.'

'If you told this story in a book, Ted, nobody would believe it. They would say it is too far-fetched.'

'There's more sir.'

Williams sat back in his chair.

'When I was looking at flight manifestos I broadened the parameters and discovered that a certain person of interest flew into the country a couple of days before the priest was murdered and this same person left the UK later on the day of the murder.'

'Don't tell me, Ted.' Williams took another sip.

'I'm afraid so, sir. Dennis McMillan is the man who I believe has attempted to murder Oxford on two separate occasions now. I'm fairly certain that the priest's death was one of mistaken identity.'

'The proper channels will have to be followed Ted. Instead of submitting a report to the Crown Prosecution Service I'll arrange for you to attend their offices and speak directly to one of the top men. Well done Ted.'

Two days later Detective Sergeant Ted Fuller took the underground service to St James Tube station and walked round the corner into Petty France and to the offices of the Crown Prosecution Service. After undergoing a rigorous security check he was handed a newly made-up plastic name badge and was taken to the office of one of the chief prosecutors.

The elderly man sat behind a desk larger than that of Detective Superintendent Williams. No whisky was produced on this occasion The ageing representative of the Crown was overweight and flushed. He had thin wispy grey hair which attempted to do its best to cover a balding crown.

Two leather upholstered chairs faced the man. One was occupied by a man in his forties. He was dressed immaculately from head to toe. His honed figure exuded confidence.

Ted Fuller was invited to take the vacant seat.

Mr 'Immaculate' was introduced as the barrister who would be leading the case for the Crown against the defendant Albert Oxford at subsequent hearings.

Ted Fuller was invited to repeat what he had told Detective Superintendent Williams. Mr 'Immaculate' took notes with an expensive looking gold-coloured fountain pen.

At the end of his story the main man from the Crown thanked Ted for his trouble. He was summarily dismissed and after handing in his lapel name badge he returned to his office at the police station.

37.

Albert had received a message from the prison adminis-
tration. He was to be taken to the Central Criminal
Court, known as the Old Bailey, the following morning.
This had taken him by surprise, as earlier he had heard
from Perkins, (Rumpole of the Bailey) that it would be
some weeks before any Court case was scheduled.

Albert asked his cellmate Edward, what this could possibly mean.

'Something's happened Albert. It may be a hearing just
so that you can enter a plea. My advice is to listen to your
barrister and do what he says. Speak to the office here to
make sure that your best clothes are available.'

Albert didn't sleep that night and was up early. He
couldn't face any breakfast as his nerves were shattered. He
washed and shaved and put on his best bib and tucker.

A prison officer came to collect him and he was placed
into one of the tight confined spaces on the prison van.
The journey to central London was again an uncomfortable trip. This was not helped by the driver of the prison
van who had a heavy right boot and made a meal out of
braking sharply. If he didn't know better Albert thought

that this was probably deliberate.

On arrival at the big brown-bricked court house in the City of London, Albert was able to spot through the barred windows of his compartment the scales of justice sitting atop the dome. Albert wondered what way the scales would tip.

In the cells of the court, built in the basement of the building, Albert was visited by Perkins. Perkins was accompanied by a barrister. He was dressed in a three-piece suit and was also wearing the black gown of his office. In his hand he held a curled white horse-hair wig. The pristine whiteness of the wig suggested that the young barrister was inexperienced and fairly new to the job.

Perkins introduced the young barrister as Charles Fielding. He grabbed Albert's hand and shook it firmly. Albert was surprised at the strength of his grip.

'Good morning Mr Oxford. Mr Perkins here, has instructed my chambers and I've been given the brief. I have read through the case notes and my belief is that this case will not get to the jury stage as there is a distinct lack of evidence and a mass of circumstantial evidence.'

'What's happening today?' Albert asked.

'The situation today is that the prosecution have asked for a hearing before the trial judge. Normally my opponent will confide in me and impart advance information to me in the robing room but in this case he has kept his cards close to his chest. We will just have to wait and see what develops when we get into court.'

Albert climbed up the stone steps. The corridor from the cells was poorly lit. Albert wondered how many infamous people had made this short journey.

He blinked as he appeared into the light of the amphitheatre. He was escorted by a uniformed prison officer and they stood in a glass walled dock facing Lord Justice Greening.

The judge was clothed in rich red robes and wore a longer white wig than those worn by the barristers.

The glass-walled dock sat in an elevated position in the middle of the courtroom. To his left were two empty benches save for bright red cushions. Albert presumed that those benches would normally contain members of a jury.

The judge sat below a huge judicial crest. He peered through rimless glasses at Albert as the clerk of the court asked Albert to confirm his name. Once he had done this Albert and his guard sat down.

Albert looked down to his right and saw in the well of the court a gathering of legal types. Albert spotted his barrister Charles Fielding sitting in front of his solicitor Perkins, who looked unusually smart. Fielding and Perkins were deep in conversation.

To their right stood a bewigged barrister who introduced himself to the judge as the Queen's Counsel appearing in this case for the prosecution.

'Yes Mr Wigg,' said the judge, 'I believe you want to address me on certain matters.'

'I do my Lord, and with your consent I will move straight into the matter in hand.'

'Carry on Mr Wigg.'

'Your Lordship, Albert Oxford appears before you this morning on a charge of murder. The circumstances are that Michael Creaney, a Catholic priest, was murdered in his church. The defendant was the beneficiary of an act of kindness by the priest in that he was offered accommodation by Father Creaney when Oxford himself had been the intended victim of an attempt on his own life.'

'On the day of the priest's death, the priest and the defendant had been heard to argue. The weapon used to kill the priest contained forensic evidence linked to Albert Oxford. Blood belonging to the victim was found on the defendant's clothing. The prosecution concedes that the evidence against Oxford is not the strongest but the Crown Prosecution Service decided that this was a case which was suitable to place before a jury, especially after examining the defendant's chequered past.'

'I have a feeling, Mr Wigg, that you are nearing the point with which you would wish to address me.'

'Indeed my Lord. The prosecution have received a report which would now jeopardise a safe conviction in this case and the prosecution are seeking permission from your Lordship to discontinue this case against Mr Oxford.'

Albert's heart missed a beat. His mouth was dry. He thought he was going to faint. The booming voice of the high-court judge concentrated his focus and attention.

'Mr Oxford, you have heard what has been said. You will be taken back downstairs and I want to see Mr Wigg and Mr Fielding in my chambers as soon as I rise.'

The court usher cried out,

'All stand.'

Albert stood alongside his prison guard. The judge stood. He bowed to the court and retired through heavy draped red curtains held apart by a court usher.

Albert walked down the steps back to his cell. He sat on the bench and couldn't allow himself to get too excited until he had spoken to Fielding and Perkins.

Perkins arrived alone. He sat on the cell bench next to Albert.

'There's been a late development. Our barrister is with the judge and prosecuting counsel but I've a feeling that the prosecution case has collapsed. I've asked for us to be supplied with a mug of tea and I'll wait here with you until Mr Fielding arrives.'

The prison orderly supplied two mugs of tea and shortly afterwards Mr Fielding arrived. He was holding his wig. Albert stood up in anticipation.

'Mr Oxford, you and I both know that the case against you was very weak but the prosecution had been determined to proceed and attempt to put your case before a jury, as flimsy as it was. However there has been a major development which has caused them to throw in the towel and, after formalities have been completed, you will be a free man. Unfortunately these formalities take time and you will have to spend another evening as a guest of Her Majesty at her fine establishment at Belmarsh.'

'I'm grateful, Mr Fielding. Can I ask what the development was that caused the prosecution to change its mind?'

'The Metropolitan Police submitted a report to the Crown Prosecution Service. This report threw serious doubt on your case and in actual fact pointed the finger of suspicion at another party.'

'Can I ask who that other party might be, sir?'

'You can ask Mr Oxford, but I'm not at liberty to say.'

38.

Albert Oxford was returned to Belmarsh Prison in the prison van. This time the lack of suspension in the vehicle did not trouble Albert as he was excited about his imminent release from Belmarsh. What did concern him however, was the thought that at least two people had attempted to kill him. His good friend, Michael Creaney, had been killed in what Albert was convinced was a murder perpetrated with mistaken identity being at the fore. Albert was now convinced that he had been the intended target at the church on that fateful night.

On being returned to his cell he told his cellmate Edward his good news. Edward was genuinely pleased for him and even more pleased when Albert offered him his supply of soap and toothpaste once his release had taken place.

Albert did not find sleep easy on that last night, tossing and turning and constantly going over in his mind who, in the outside world, was trying to eliminate him.

Could it be the gangs whose paths he had crossed previously, seeking their revenge? At least seven of them were now dead. Then he thought about Cronk, the retired detective who had journeyed to Spain and who had shot Albert in the head and whom he had presumed to be dead before turning the gun on himself. Did Cronk have an accomplice?

Eventually Albert drifted off into a sleep punctuated by dreams of deeds most foul.

When morning eventually arrived, Albert washed and donned his civvy clothes which had been brought to the cell. He ignored breakfast. Edward was pleased with the extra rations and after finishing his tea and an awkward man-hug with Edward, Albert was escorted to the main reception area where he signed for the property that had been taken from him when he had first arrived at the prison. He was given a sum of money on release and details of hostels for ex-prisoners.

He stepped out through the side prison door into the luke-warm sunshine and made his way to the bus stop on the other side of the road. He eventually made his way to Stoke Newington where he looked up the hostel that had been recommended to him.

Albert presented himself to the warden who went through all the rules and regulations. He was taken to a cubicle which contained a bed and a chest of drawers. There was no Bible in the top drawer.

At the end of the corridor was situated a communal washroom which had towels of varying degrees of grubbiness available for use.

Albert tested his bed. It was uncomfortable but would be a place to sleep. His escort, the warden, said that he would soon get used to the smells and odours of unwashed bodies. He said the noise was also off-putting but added that he would soon get used to that as well. Albert vowed that he was going to spend as little time as possible in this place.

39.

Albert had decided that he was going to pay a visit to St Paul's Church. He approached tentatively, not knowing what to expect.

The main front door to the church was closed and obviously not open for business. Albert saw that the door to the late Father Creaney's living quarters was slightly ajar. He knocked. The big frame of Thomas Cannon appeared and both men beamed at each other.

'How are you Albert?'

'I'm fine now that I'm out of that Belmarsh place. The Crown Prosecution Service has dropped the case against me and I've just been to a hostel which is worse than Belmarsh.'

'I'm pleased you're out, Albert. I've been sleeping here in Father's quarters. The Church authorities asked me to keep an eye on the place until the new man arrives. You're welcome to share if you like.'

'That's very nice of you Thomas, but I'm going to look at the possibility of using my canal boat again. It's been a while since I've been down there for obvious reasons. But first I'll need my keys to the boat.'

'Not a problem Albert. I cleared your living quarters out and your clothes and other stuff are in the little room off the kitchen here. If you like, I can come down to the boat with you. I could do with a change of scenery.'

Albert picked up his boat keys and with Thomas they jumped aboard a single decker bus which travelled past Hackney Marshes. They alighted at the stop nearest the River Lea Navigation canal and walked along the towpath which led past the cavernous bowl that was the London Stadium.

As Albert approached the canal boat that was his home, he couldn't help thinking about his boat companion Bart, his trusted Jack Russell. He saw Kevin and Caroline, his boat neighbours on the deck of their boat tending to their potted plant display. They looked pleased to see Albert but asked Albert where his dog was. Albert told them his sad news and introduced Thomas as a friend of his.

Albert opened up the boat. A stale smell pervaded the air. The windows were opened, and with Thomas's help Albert cleaned and washed the deck area and cleaned all the surfaces. He emptied his canvas carry bag and restored his radio to its rightful position next to the boat cabin bed.

'I think it's time for me to buy you a pint, Thomas. Thanks for your help. It was difficult coming back here and the next big test is to gauge the reaction from the Plume of Feathers.'

'You won't have a problem there Albert. Nobody believes for one minute that you were responsible for the death of our friend.'

As Albert and Thomas approached the public house

from the bus stop Albert wondered what sort of reception he would receive from the regulars in the bar. On entering he saw that a few of the patrons were sitting in their usual positions, either supping from a pint glass or participating in a game of dominoes. Two punters were throwing darts at a dartboard.

The pub fell silent when Albert walked through the door but after a pregnant pause he was welcomed enthusiastically by all those in the bar.

Albert couldn't help noticing an unframed photograph of Father Creaney pinned to the wall above his customary chair. The photograph showed Michael Creaney cradling a pint of guinness. The chair remained unoccupied.

Albert ordered two pints for himself and Thomas and during the course of the next two hours Albert became aware of a sense of fury and injustice. The regulars were upset that Michael Creaney's killer was still at large.

Later, when Albert was back inside the cabin of his canal boat he reflected on the situation. Cronk had attempted to kill him in Spain before taking his own life. Somebody, as yet unknown, had attempted to kill him twice since his return to the UK. Unfortunately, this had resulted in the death of his friend in a case of mistaken identity. Albert now made a commitment to himself that he would avow the death of his friend.

His first port of call the following day would be to speak to Detective Sergeant Fuller, the CID officer who had investigated the attempt on his life on the canal boat.

40.

The following morning, Albert rang Hackney police station and asked the receptionist to be put through to Detective Sergeant Fuller. Fuller answered the phone and Albert said to him,

'I need to speak to you about the shooting that took place on the River Lea Navigation Canal.

Fuller replied, 'There's a cafe in Lower Clapton Road next to the mosque. I'll see you there in 30 minutes. I'll have a mug of tea with two sugars.' Albert smiled to himself and set off for the cafe.

Next to the mosque was a brightly painted greasy-spoon cafe run by a large West Indian man sporting a headful of Rastafarian dreadlocks. The cafe advertised all day breakfasts for £4.50.

Albert entered the cafe and sat at the back. He read a newspaper which had kindly been left by the previous occupant of the seat he now sat in. He ordered himself a strong coffee and intimated to the young black waitress that a mug of tea with two sugars would be required shortly.

Fuller entered the cafe five minutes later and picked up

his mug from the counter and sat down opposite Albert.

'Now, you said on the phone that you wanted to talk to me about the attempt on your life.'

'That's right,' said Albert. 'I think I'm entitled to know who's trying to kill me and why.'

'That's why I'm here.'

'Why couldn't you tell me over the telephone?' asked Albert with a puzzled frown.

'I'll come to that in a minute, but I know that you have previous convictions for tape-recording conversations and there is sensitive information I wish to relay to you but before I do, I need to know that you're not wired up or recording this.'

'Mr Fuller, you can trust me.'

Fuller smiled but asked Albert to open his jacket and lift up his shirt. Satisfied that Albert was not recording the conversation Fuller said,

'Thank you, Mr Oxford.'

'Now that you trust me you can call me Albert if you like.'

'Okay Albert,' said Fuller with the merest trace of a smile. 'My enquiries into the attempt on your life were fruitful. The gunman left his car near the changing rooms at the Marshes. From CCTV footage I was able to identify the make and number of the vehicle. The vehicle was registered to William Cronk.'

Albert gasped, 'The nutter who tried to kill me in Spain?'

'The very one, and, as both of us are astute detectives, we can safely assume that it was not Cronk who attempted to kill you on your canal boat.'

'You've got more obviously?'

'I have. The car was circulated as a vehicle of interest and was subsequently found abandoned in a multi-storey car park in Stratford. A fingerprint was found in a compromising place and a search on this print showed that it belonged to a retired police officer who was a close associate of Cronk. We also found the rifle that had been used but that was clean of prints.

'Can I ask who this person was? 'said Albert.

'The name wouldn't mean anything to you Albert, but let me continue. I checked all the flight itineraries for planes arriving at London airports just before the shooting and for the thirty six hours following the shootings and this name cropped up.'

'So this maniac has been arrested?' asked Albert.

'Unfortunately no. The powers that be informed me that there wasn't sufficient evidence to justify a trip to Spain to interview this suspect.' Fuller paused and sipped his tea.

'There's more to come I suspect,' said Albert.

'There is. When your recently departed landlord, the Irish priest, was murdered, I was informed that you had been arrested. I then resorted to checking flight itineraries again and lo and behold the same name cropped up as flying into Stansted two days before the murder and leaving the country within twenty four hours on a flight bound for Spain, and Alicante in particular.'

'I take it then that the target in the chapel was meant to be me?' asked Albert.

'That's right and as a result of that information I submitted a report to the authorities at the Crown Prosecution

Service and they decided, rightly, that a prosecution and conviction against you would be unsafe.'

'And as a result of that I was released from Belmarsh?'

'That's correct. You owe me Albert, but I will settle for another mug of tea.'

Albert caught the eye of the waitress and beckoned on her to top up their empty mugs.

Once the mugs had been replenished Fuller continued,

'The suspect obviously lives in Spain and works as a private investigator. He has been flagged up to the Spanish Guardia but enquiries show that he has disappeared and is hiding-up somewhere. That is the position as it stands and I felt I owed it to you to tell you what has happened.'

'So you're telling me Sergeant Fuller, that this assassin is somewhere in Spain. He's attempted to kill me and murdered an innocent Irish priest who wouldn't hurt a fly and he's as free as a bird and nobody can do anything about it?'

Fuller could see that Albert was getting hot under the collar and losing it a bit.

'Once the Spanish police have located our suspect I'll fly to Spain to interview him and initiate extradition processes to bring him back to this country with a view to him standing trial for the murder of Michael Creaney and the attempt on your life.'

'That could take months, or even years,' replied Albert.

Fuller nodded in agreement.

'What is the name of this creature?' asked Albert.

'His name is Dennis Charles McMillan,' replied the detective.

When they left the cafe Fuller walked off in the direction of his police station. Albert decided to walk back to the church and on his walk he struggled to control his temper and his emotions. He thought he had left all that behind him but now was more determined than ever to hunt down this killer and seek revenge on behalf of the Catholic priest.

He walked into the living quarters of the church and sat at the table and spoke to Thomas. He told Thomas the whole conversation he had had with Fuller. Albert could see that Thomas was angry at the fact that McMillan had appeared to get away with murder.

'Albert, I think you and I should have a little holiday. Spain sounds like a good place to be at this time of year.'

Albert smiled for the first time since his meeting with Fuller in the cafe.

'The problem Thomas, is finding McMillan. It will be like looking for a needle in a haystack. We will need money. My resources are limited and it might take us ages to find him. We might not even find him.'

'Albert, we need to give it a try. We've nothing to lose. I'll have to think about finances but I'm sure we will get support from the clientele at the pub and from some of the church-goers.'

'I admire your optimism Thomas but I'm not as confident as you.'

41.

ennis McMillan was not a happy soul. Although he still had a source of income through his official vocation as a private investigator, his most lucrative source of finance was from his drug running exploits. This money had paid for his pleasures in life. He now saw that this was being taken away from him. He was convinced that the drug running gig had been handed to the duplicitous Mateo. McMillan vowed to get even with his former pupil.

McMillan was also embarrassed by his failure to kill Albert Oxford. Oxford had got lucky on the first attempt but McMillan now knew he had messed things up badly on his second attempt. This had resulted in the unfortunate death of an innocent man.

He also was concerned that the female detective, Webster, knew all about his failed attempts. Could he trust her? All of this added to McMillan's inner rage.

McMillan left a note for his wife saying he was going away for a few days. No doubt she would be pleased. McMillan then packed two canvas bags full of essentials. He emptied his floor safe of a considerable amount of euros and then drove to the coast where he had his small motor-boat moored.

He figured that if Mateo was now the drug runner he wouldn't be using the same moorings as himself so McMillan decided on a plan to visit the harbours and marinas in the direction of where it would be easier to access the drug packages and bhoys.

His plan would take some time to execute but patience was one of the strong points required in the business of private investigation.

The next harbour was only five kilometres south of where his own boat was moored. He approached the office of the harbour master and flashed his investigator's licence at the small stocky Spaniard. He looked unimpressed by the credentials but was more impressed by the twenty euro note which McMillan had produced. A glance through the registered boat owners on this log did not produce the name that McMillan was looking for.

McMillan moved on to the next port of call. A similar strategy produced another blank result. The next harbour produced a result insomuch as McMillan did not have to part with twenty euros but was once again negative as far as Mateo was concerned.

At the next marina McMillan struck gold. Mateo's name jumped out at him from the register. McMillan was careful not to identify the target but shrugged his shoulders to indicate that there was nothing in the register that was of any assistance to him. McMillan had noted the berth number allocated to Mateo's small boat.

Scanning the small picturesque harbour, McMillan noted a number of boats bobbing about in the small rippled waves. He calculated where the berth was that his target was moored to and was happy to see that a small boat with a motor engine attached was secured to two rings. It was covered with a tarpaulin.

McMillan's next move was to find a cheap Spanish motel. This was some way into the town away from the coast but was perfect for McMillan as he could park his SEAT vehicle in the dust bowl of a car park under the shade of a tree. He would be able to work on his computer through the day and keep observation on the boat and its owner at night. This night time work would also enable McMillan to catch up on his sleep through the day when he wasn't working the keyboard of his computer.

42.

Albert and Thomas entered the Plume of feathers and both were greeted warmly. The friends of the late Michael Creaney were incensed by the needless killing of the priest. There was much talk of revenge.

Thomas updated the group on the person responsible and the fact that he had disappeared back to Spain and the added information that attempts to find and locate him would take some time. The mood was rebellious and loud. Albert had never seen the regulars so animated before.

As more and more alcohol flowed, all sorts of plans were mooted, some bordering on the ridiculous and farcical. Albert sat and listened to it all. If the official arm of the law was powerless to extradite McMillan, what chance did the dominoes team of the Plume of Feathers have?

Albert looked across at Thomas and he appeared to be equally despondent. Albert finished his pint and decided to walk back through Hackney to the canal boat. He said his good-byes and stepped out into the cool evening air.

Albert walked along the main road which cut through to Hackney Marshes. As the road ran out of houses and was replaced by open green spaces and trees he became aware that he had been overtaken by a large black shiny Bentley. It came to a stop about fifty yards beyond him.

A powerfully built male unfurled himself from the front passenger seat. He was wearing a smart dark suit and black roll-neck and sported crew-cut black hair. Albert guessed that he would be a handful if the situation turned violent. The man waited until Albert was level with the rear of the car and said,

'Albert Oxford?'

'That's me. Who's asking?'

'My boss would like a word with you. He's sitting in the back of the motor. But before you get into the car I want to check you are not carrying anything that you shouldn't have.'

Albert didn't see the point of arguing and raised his arms. The minder frisked Albert. He tried to peer into the back of the vehicle but the tinted windows prevented him from seeing the occupant.

Once satisfied that Albert was clean, the minder opened the rear door of the Bentley. In the spacious rear seat sat a smartly dressed man. Albert guessed he was aged in his mid fifties. His black suit was cut from the finest cloth and he was wearing a plain white shirt with a starched collar. A dark blue tie was pinned to his shirt with what looked like a diamond encrusted tie-pin. The man was clean shaven with short grey hair. His cuff-links sparkled in the low light of the car's interior illumination. His after-shave was subtle and obviously expensive.

Albert saw that there was another minder behind the steering wheel. He could easily have passed off as an identical twin to the first minder who had approached Albert.

Albert went to sit in the rear seat next to the man. He sank into the plush leather seat.

'You two can take a short walk for a bit. I want to have a private chat with Mr Oxford.' The soft voice had the faintest trace of an Irish accent.

The two minders stepped out of the car and strolled off down the road.

'Mr Oxford, my name is Aidan Doyle. I want to talk to you about Michael Creaney.'

Doyle pressed a button on the central console between the two rear seats. A walnut facia door lowered from the panel in front of them and revealed a drinks cabinet situated behind the driver's seat.

'Will you join me, Mr Oxford'

Doyle placed two fine cut-glass tumblers on the tray and from a decanter poured a liberal measure into each glass.

'Bushmills Irish whiskey. I haven't found anything to beat it.'

'Thank you, Mr Doyle.'

Albert sipped from his glass and had to agree that it was indeed a very fine whiskey.

'I'm going to tell you about myself, some things which I haven't told anyone else. I was born in a small town in the Republic of Ireland many years ago. I went to a school in that town and my best friend was Michael Creaney. We were inseperable. We both played a multitude of sports, we also fished together, and as we grew older our friendship grew stronger.

170

'Michael decided as a young man that his future lay with God. He studied hard and found immense happiness as one of God's advocates. My career took a different path. I decided at an early age that money would provide my happiness. Two very contrasting life-styles, you might think?'

Albert nodded.

'Although we had chosen different career paths our friendship remained strong. I made my money in the financial institutions of the City of London and this enabled me to pursue my love of the sport of horse-racing. I have various bloodstock interests in Ireland as well as a thriving stud. Michael was a frequent visitor and we were able to indulge in our love of fishing, Guinness and fine food. Michael was a frequent guest of mine in my private box at the Cheltenham Festival as well as accompanying me to the big meetings at Aintree and Epsom.

'Throughout his various postings as a priest I have maintained contact with him and visited him on numerous occasions at his places of work. So, you can imagine my crushing sadness at the news of his death, especially when I found out that you were the intended target.'

Albert felt a bit uneasy and wondered to himself where this was going.

'Michael told me that he enjoyed your company and that you had even introduced him to the complexities of the game of cricket, a God forsaken sport if you ask me. He enjoyed your company and trusted you, despite your chequered past.'

'You seem to know quite a bit about me Mr Doyle.'

'I do, Mr Oxford. I have made it my business to find out

everything about you and the possible suspect. The suspect is now resident in Spain and is currently evading the clutches of the Spanish Police.'

Albert took another sip of the Bushmills and mused that Doyle was very well informed and realised that he had obviously been fed this information by Detective Sergeant Fuller and that it was just as obvious that it had been Fuller who had supplied Doyle with his details.

'This suspect, who we will call Dennis Charles McMillan, for that is his name, has attempted to kill you on two occasions. McMillan has executed my very close friend Father Creaney and I know that you were very close to Michael so I suspect that apart from seeking revenge for the attempts on your own life that you might be anxious to avenge the death of Michael Creaney. How am I doing so far?'

'I can't argue with anything you have said,' replied Albert.

'This is the position. May I call you Albert?'

'Of course,' Albert replied.

'Because I have the means, I'm quite prepared to finance you in your efforts to even the score. For purely personal reasons I want my name kept out of everything. My business depends on my reputation. Do you have any game plan in mind?'

'I do, but I haven't got the resources required. My intention would be to get to McMillan's part of Spain and have him topped. I have a friend who would accompany me on the trip but obviously accommodation and working expenses wouldn't come cheap.'

'I understand that,' replied Doyle, 'and that's where I come in. On production of a working plan, of which I have to approve, I will finance your expedition. It will be cash only, part Euros and part sterling, to keep the job as clean as possible. You will have a guardian angel on this side of the water who is in my employ and who will help where he can.'

Albert surmised that this angel would be in the form of Ted Fuller.

'In the meantime I would be obliged if within a couple of days you attend my offices in the Barbican and speak to one of these protection officers and appraise them of your plan.'

Doyle gave Albert a plain white business card on which was printed an address and a telephone number.

The two minders returned to the vehicle as if they had been mysteriously summoned by remote control.

One of the minders opened Albert's door. Albert nodded at Doyle and they shook hands.

On the walk back to his canal boat Albert could not contain his excitement and eagerly looked forward to speaking with Thomas the next morning.

Albert could not get to sleep but eventually the gentle rocking of the boat and the sound of the tiny waves lapping up against the hull sent him off into a deep sleep.

43.

Now that McMillan knew where Mateo moored his small craft, it was only a matter of time before Mateo ventured out to sea to collect the package from the depths of the Mediterranean.

McMillan was prepared to be patient and had plotted himself up in a small cafe sitting just by the northern end of the marina. McMillan knew that he didn't have to spot Mateo leaving in his motor boat but he knew roughly how long the exercise would take and he could then plan his surprise for Mateo on his return.

On the fourth day of observation, just as dusk was beginning to settle on the seaside village, McMillan noticed that the motorboat was missing from its mooring. McMillan had calculated how long the collection and return would take so he took the opportunity to catch up on sleep as he knew that he would be busy well into the night.

Mateo had slipped the securing ropes and steered his small craft out to sea. When working with McMillan, McMillan had always thought it was a two-man job but Mateo was convinced that he would be able to handle this on his own as he was fit and strong enough and had always done the donkey work whilst McMillan had supervised. Mateo had checked the coordinates on his mobile and set off in that direction. The sea was calm allowing him to make smooth progress.

In the distance Mateo spotted the intermittent flashing light on the marker buoy. He slowed the boat to a virtual standstill and secured his craft to the buoy with a substantial length of heavy chain.

Once that had been done, Mateo set about the strenuous task of hauling the heavily wrapped package into his boat. The task was not as easy as he had thought, but eventually, after thirty minutes of straining and pulling the package had been landed.

Mateo released the heavy securing chain and stowed it near the bow of the boat. He then guided his boat back to the safety of the harbour marina he had left some hours earlier.

McMillan sat on one of the benches along the harbour wall. In the stillness of the night he thought he could hear the chug-chug of a small motor boat. Sure enough, appearing in view was the small craft with Mateo at the helm, steering his boat to the far side of the marina where he had parked the fish van that would take the package of drugs to the person further up the chain of command in this drug cartel.

He secured his boat temporarily whilst he manhandled the heavy package to the rear doors of his van.

Mateo heard a clatter of footsteps and turned round suddenly to see Dennis McMillan brandishing a claw hammer.

Mateo only felt the first blow across his forehead. There followed two more blows which accounted for the short life of Mateo.

McMillan half carried and half dragged the lifeless body back to his craft moored to the ring on the jetty. McMillan covered the body in the boat with a tarpaulin. He then returned to his own vehicle, the SEAT Leon estate car which he parked next to the fish van. The package was transferred to his vehicle and covered from view.

McMillan returned to Mateo's motor boat and used the length of chain to bind him. He started up the boat and steered out to sea.

After sailing for a couple of miles, McMillan checked that the chain wrapped around the body was secure. He picked up the lifeless package and tipped it over the side of the boat. A ripple of air bubbles broke the calm surface of the sea, and then the stream of bubbles ceased. Satisfied that the chained corpse had sunk to the bottom of the Mediterranean, McMillan steered the craft back to its mooring.

His work for that night was still not complete, as the package in the car, if discovered, would compromise McMillan. He had a plan. He drove in the direction of his cheap motel. On the way he pulled off the road onto a narrow track which he had identified on an earlier reconnaissance mission. This track eventually led to a large copse of trees with a small clearing in the middle.

McMillan spent the next ninety minutes digging a hole in the ground large enough to accommodate the package. The digging was complicated by the abundance of tree roots but eventually McMillan was satisfied with his labours. The package was deposited and re-covered with soil. McMillan made a half decent attempt to restore the ground to looking like it was undisturbed.

Dawn was about to break as McMillan drove back to his temporary accommodation.

44.

'The kettle's just boiled,' said Thomas Cannon as Albert appeared through the door of the kitchen.

Albert had walked to the church of St Paul from his canal boat. There was a spring in his step. He couldn't wait to tell Thomas his news.

Albert now sat at the kitchen table with a mug of strong tea. Thomas sensed he was itching to tell him something important.

'How do you feel about the killing of Michael Creaney?' asked Albert.

Thomas sat silently for a few seconds and replied,

'During my career with my unit in the Middle East and Northern Ireland I witnessed some terrible atrocities and I've lost many good friends, but this has affected me more than any of those acts. The man, Michael, was a very good friend to me and saved my life by digging me out of the hell hole I was in. I've vowed to myself that I'll do whatever I can do to get back at the bastard who's done this.'

'I feel guilty about all of this Thomas, as I was the intended victim.'

'You've nothing to be feeling guilty about Albert. You've

178

been a great friend to me recently as well, and I'm just as angry with this animal for targeting you.'

'The suspect is known to the police Thomas, but the killer's fled back to Spain. He's been a resident there for a few years and has a job there. The detective who was investigating the attempt on my life on the canal has done a lot of digging and found that this bloke entered the country at the time of my shooting and re-entered the country just a couple of days before Father Creaney was brutally murdered.'

'I presume plod are in the process of extraditing the suspect?' asked Thomas.

'No, unfortunately not,' replied Albert, 'which only means one thing.'

Thomas's face broke into a huge grin.

'That can only mean that we have to do the job ourselves. Once he's been capped we won't have to bring him back here.'

'Exactly my thoughts,' replied Albert.

'We need to think about finance, Albert, and it might take more than the two of us.'

'The finances are not a problem, now. I met up last night with a very good friend of Michael Creaney. He's caked up with cash and is anxious that some form of justice is enacted. You don't need to know who he is, Thomas, but I'll handle that side of things. You'll need to have to think about who we take with us.'

'I've already got at least one person in mind, Albert. You remember Brendan who was sleeping in a shop doorway. The one who gifted us the Albanian muggers. He's fallen on hard times and the government has abandoned those who served in the cause of this country. His mental health issues are minor but he'd jump at the opportunity to get involved in something like this.'

'He'd need a wash and brush-up,' said Albert, smiling. 'Was he part of your old unit?'

'He was, and he was a great operator. There is not a thing he doesn't know about engines and mechanics. He's also fairly adept with explosives and killing people.'

'Seems perfect for the job,' smiled Albert. 'Has he got a passport and driving licence?'

'Yeh, they'll be in storage at his younger sister's place. And before you ask, he couldn't stay with her as she has a young family and she worried about Brendan's mental stability.'

'Did you have anyone else in mind Thomas?'

'I do, and the bonus is that he's already based in Spain. He speaks good enough Spanish, which might be useful, and his expertise lies with firearms and explosives. He doesn't know anything about this yet obviously, but he was also part of the old unit and he will be with us like a shot when I tell him what we are proposing.'

'Sounds great. I have given it a little bit of thought and to cut down on expenses I intend to long-rent a comfortable motor-home. We can travel down in that and use it as a base for our operation. It can be parked up in these caravan rest places.'

'Do we know what part of Spain we're heading for?' asked Thomas.

'Not yet, but I have a friendly face in the old bill who

wants to help us without showing out too much. The financier and him have already been in touch with each other if my thinking is correct.'

'When do we leave Albert?'

'As soon as I have obtained the motorhome and the money.' replied Albert.

Albert went to clear away the empty mugs of tea and couldn't help thinking about Helen who would normally have been here tidying up.

'Did you say that Helen's gone back to Ireland?' asked Albert.

'She has Albert. The church personnel who are overseeing Michael's replacement said that Helen wanted to attend Michel's funeral in his little village but because of Covid restrictions she couldn't go. Her village and Michael's are not a million miles apart.'

Albert was pleased to hear that she had been able to be repatriated to her part of Ireland. As well as missing the priest, he also missed the sereneness and beauty of the ex-nun. He had never been happier recently when he and Helen had taken the dogs to the park for a walk. That was all gone now, thanks to McMillan. Albert felt the rage rise within himself.

If it was the last thing he ever did, it would be to rid this world of Dennis McMillan.

45.

Although the Spanish sun shone brightly there was a darkness that hung over the village of Passina. The ordinary law-abiding villagers were fearful of the crime boss El Poderoso. He and his thugs ran the village and surrounding towns with a fist of iron.

Not one of the villagers had the temerity to challenge the nasty piece of work as they had witnessed, or heard about what fate had befallen those who had been brave enough to try. Their lives therefore, were spent avoiding contact with him or his gang and minding their own business.

Just off the village square where El Poderoso lived, was situated a cafe. It had the appearance of a traveller's stop. Outside the cafe there was sprinkled an assortment of formica topped tables, some of which had been covered with a bright shiny plastic table covering. The doorway to the cafe led to a small bar with tables and chairs placed near the windows.

A barman quietly went about his business, cleaning glasses which had previously contained fruit juices or the local Spanish beer. Behind the plastic screen on the counter was a display of freshly made sandwiches, tortilla and other snacks.

The barman suddenly looked up from his cleaning duties. His attention was drawn to a flurry of activity outside the cafe as two large saloon cars with darkened windows slid to a halt near the tables. The two cars were followed by a motor-cycle and pillion passenger and the rear of the convoy was completed by a flat-bed truck which contained three middle aged men all wearing dark clothing.

The cars disgorged their passengers and the troupe of hoodlums entered through the front door of the cafe.

The barman knew what was now expected of him. He retired to the back of the restaurant with a set of keys and opened a door set into the wall at the rear of the bar area. He opened this door and allowed the men through into a room which had always impressed him with its elegance and beauty.

The finest furniture had been used to form a classical looking restaurant. The tables had been set with fine linen table-cloths and laid with expensive cutlery. Cut-glass wine glasses were placed near the settings. Heavy draped maroon curtains kept out the natural light but this had been replaced by subtle ceiling lights which were controlled at the entry door by a dimmer switch.

The entourage swept into this classical restaurant and the barman waited with some trepidation to take orders for food and drink. He was relieved that the only order of the day was for strong coffee. Once that had been done he stationed himself by the bar waiting for further orders. The bell on the counter would summon him to waiting duties.

The one person that the barman was careful not to upset

was the small, nasty looking individual who constantly wore a blue cashmere scarf. He wondered how someone of his stunted stature could wield so much power but he had heard some horror stories of his cruelty to women and children in the village. Men who had upset him tended to be never seen again.

The meeting in the restaurant did not last long. The Council had been addressed by El Poderoso. He threatened them and demanded that the missing Mateo be found and executed. Just as important, he had added, was the recovery of the drugs which he now knew had been collected. He gave them a list of tasks.

His last job now was to contact El Caballo to inform him that McMillan was now a person not to be trusted. He told El Caballo that he could earn his respect if he eliminated McMillan. He also told him that McMillan had stolen the latest consignment of high-end drugs and that their safe return would further elevate El Caballo's position

After the telephone call El Poderoso noted to himself that the Horse did not sound pleased with this latest instruction.

46.

Albert took the London Underground to Liverpool Street station and decided to walk to the address in the Barbican. The impressive block of offices towered above the streets.

Albert walked into the reception area and spoke to a smart suited young man behind a glass facade. Albert told him his name and he was immediately issued with a name-tagged pass. He noted that it just said 'OXFORD'. The young receptionist pointed to a bank of lifts and told him to ask for the eighteenth floor where he would be met on exiting the lift.

At the eighteenth floor Albert was indeed met by another smartly dressed operative who looked as if he could handle himself. He led Albert down a heavily carpeted corridor towards an oak door. The man used a plastic fob to gain entry. The oak-panelled room was small but the glass external wall afforded spectacular views of the city of London's skyline. The only furniture in the room was a rectangular wooden oak table on which was placed a black leather attache case.

The operative opened the case to reveal an amount of

Euros neatly packaged and bound in plastic. Albert noticed in the attache case a mobile phone.

'There is 40,000 euros there and 40,000 in sterling,' said the minder in a soft but clear voice. 'I will require a signature for that.'

Albert signed and dated the piece of paper which had been produced. He returned it to the suit who folded it and placed it in his inside jacket pocket. As he did this Albert noticed that he was wearing a shoulder holster which contained a handgun. Doyle is obviously a serious operator, thought Albert.

'The mobile phone's a burner phone,' said the suit. 'It should only be used in the case of an extreme emergency. There's only one number plumbed in there and it shouldn't take you long to work it out who that is. You'll be ringing another burner phone. The money is to finance your trip abroad. Your sponsor doesn't want to hear from you. You should use the phone to indicate that you've succeeded in your task. Do you have any questions?'

'No, everything's pretty clear.'

Albert had been asked by Doyle to submit a plan but that had either been forgotten about or, more likely, Doyle trusted him to carry out the plan and not involve the financier in any way. In any event he left the envelope containing the plan on the table.

Albert was led back to the lifts and descended to the reception area. He handed in his pass and walked back to Liverpool Street station. He was conscious of the case that he carried and how much it contained.

At the end of his Tube journey Albert hailed a taxi which

took him to St Paul's Church. He sat with Thomas in the kitchen area and over a mug of tea he told Thomas what had happened.

'Well done Albert. It looks like we're on our way. We will need to discuss personnel and timings as well as transport.'

'I'm going to hire the motorhome tomorrow, Thomas. In the meantime you can round up Brendan, tell him to get his passport and driving licence. If he's got any spare clobber, make sure he's got it with him when he gets here. He can shower upstairs.'

'No problem. I won't tell our Spanish friend until we're about to leave. I don't want him getting too excited too early. I think you'll be impressed by him.'

'Sounds good,' smiled Albert. 'Just one other job for tomorrow Thomas. You'll need to speak to the church authorities to inform them that we're locking the place up and the premises will be vacated. You'll also need to pack a bag.'

47.

McMillan was holed up in his hotel room, fretting. He was consoled by the fact that there was nothing on the local Spanish news outlets about the disappearance of Mateo. McMillan had remained in the hotel and used it as a base as he still wasn't sure about a reaction from the crime gang boss regarding the disappearance of his courier and, more importantly, his consignment of drugs.

McMillan rang his wife to tell her that he would be on extended leave from the marital home.

'You need to be,' she said, 'the Guardia Civil have been here looking for you. What have you been up to?'

McMillan ignored her question and cut short the call.

He also missed Carmela and everything else that that involved but could not afford taking a chance on meeting up with her because of her father El Caballo, and his gang members, never mind the Spanish Police.

McMillan made the decision that he would travel to meet El Poderoso at his village headquarters.

He travelled to Passina by car. He parked just outside the village and walked to the four storey building that El Poderoso called home. A surly minder sat on a plastic chair outside the door to the building. McMillan asked if he could have a meeting with his boss but received a snarling reply that the gang leader was at his council operation centre at the cafe.

McMillan walked up the hill towards the cafe. He saw that the cafe had the appearance of a normal Spanish watering hole but he was aware that a back room had been converted into a luxurious restaurant that was only used by El Poderoso, his gang, and specially invited guests.

McMillan walked into the small bar that served the ordinary part of the cafe and catered for the occupants of the plastic chairs and tables outside on the sunny, dusty veranda.

A gun-toting guard sat outside the entrance to the restaurant. McMillan asked if he could speak to his boss. The guard looked him up and down and indicated to him to remain where he was. The guard entered the plush restaurant and after a couple of minutes returned and told McMillan to enter the restaurant.

McMillan stepped inside the heavy wooden door. The room was brightly lit but after stepping into the room all the lighting was extinguished and McMillan felt being grabbed from behind with his arms being pinned to his sides. A hood was placed over his head and secured tightly at the neck causing him to choke and gasp for breath. His wrists were secured and he was placed roughly onto a chair.

McMillan had a more than generous grasp of the Spanish language and was able to understand the questions that came his way.

'You were relieved of the job of collecting my drugs.'

McMillan nodded.

'The person to whom I gave the job has disappeared.'

'I didn't know that.'

McMillan was struck on the side of the head with a heavy object. He fell to the floor but was roughly grabbed and put back into the chair.

'What is more disturbing is that I know that the drugs have been picked up and they have also disappeared.'

McMillan thought it prudent not to answer or make any movement but that was to no avail as he received another heavy blow to the side of his head. He could feel what was obviously blood trickling down his cheek.

McMillan was about to plead his innocence but lost consciousness when a savage blow to the back of his head rendered him senseless.

His trussed body was carried out of the restaurant via the rear door. McMillan was placed in the rear of a Berlingo van and covered with sacking.

The van was driven away from the restaurant. In the back of the van McMillan regained consciousness. The van stunk of rotting vegetables and McMillan quickly realised that he was still hooded with his wrists still bound. The van was now being driven along a dirt track and McMillan felt every bump and turn.

The van came to a halt and the back doors were opened. McMillan had decided that his tactic would be to play-act that he was still comatose. He felt one of his captors untie his wrists. He let the loosened hands flop naturally. He was then carried and after a few yards was placed roughly on the ground.

His hood was removed and McMillan resisted the strong

urge to open his eyes. He felt his body being rolled over. The two guards were using their feet to roll him into a certain position.

'Adios, buen viaje'

McMillan's basic grasp of the Spanish language told him that this translated to 'Goodbye, have a good trip.'

He was rolled over an edge. He opened his eyes and in an instant realised immediately that he had been rolled over the edge of a cliff. He fell with his arms flailing, trying desperately to grab any bush or foliage to break his fall. He crashed onto an outcrop of rock and lost all feeling in his left shoulder. Pebbles that had been disturbed by his fall rained down after him.

He crashed onto the ledge which halted his momentum and with his one remaining good hand stretched out and grabbed the thorny branches of a rock plant. He was perched precariously on a narrow outcrop of rock. He looked up but could not see the top of the cliff but he treated that as good news as it meant his two escorts could not see him.

He looked down. That was probably a bad move as the sight of a 200 feet drop into a dry, rocky ravine was not very appetising. He thought about why they had removed the restraints and hood but then assumed that they had wanted his death to appear as an accident whereby a walker had obviously slipped and fell over the edge.

His immediate problem however, was what to do now. He couldn't move without the risk of falling. Because of his injured shoulder he wouldn't be able to climb up or down the rocky face of the ravine.

48.

Thomas Cannon was tidying up the kitchen of the quarters that had once been a happy place when Father Michael Creaney was alive. He had packed his bag and was waiting for Brendan to appear. As he looked out of the net curtained kitchen window Thomas smiled as he saw a shiny motorhome reversing into the parking bay next to the church. Albert was sitting proudly behind the steering wheel.

'Our new toy and our new home for our adventure,' said Albert alighting from the cab.

'I hope you've added me onto the insurance,' smiled Thomas.

Albert gave the big man a guided tour of the vehicle. There were three seats in the front of the vehicle including that of the driver. They moved through to the rear area. Albert pointed out the double bed space situated above the driver's cabin. A seated area obviously converted into another double bed and after inspecting the small sink and kitchen area they moved through to the rear of the vehicle which housed a chemical toilet and another space to accommodate a bed.

The decor was a dull beige but the surfaces were clean. Thomas and Albert examined the inner workings of the vehicle and agreed that there needed to be rules set regarding use of the chemical toilet. Designated rest areas on the continent of Europe were to be used for that purpose.

An unkempt figure appeared at the side door to the motor van.

Thomas greeted the man. Now that he was standing Albert did not at first recognise the man he had last seen sitting on a blanket in Stoke Newington. At least he had made some attempt to clean himself up but Thomas insisted that he made liberal use of the shower room in the residential quarters that had once been Albert's home.

When Brendan reappeared he was wearing a change of clothes donated to him by Thomas. Albert had cooked the three of them a brunch of eggs, bacon and sausages.

After the brunch had been devoured, Thomas set about clearing up the plates and crockery in an effort to leave the premises as tidy as they could.

'Has Thomas explained to you the details and the reasons behind our trip?' Albert asked Brendan.

'He has. As I understand it we're after a man who killed the parish priest. He was under the impression that he was killing you.'

'What's your motivation for getting involved, Brendan?'

'Two of my best friends are involved in this. Thomas has been brilliant with me over the years. He saved my life in Iraq. The other man in Spain is a hero of mine. We all served in the same unit in the Middle East. This is probably my last hurrah. Years of dossing in doorways has messed up my lungs and other vital organs so I want to go out on a high with two of my best mates.'

'Welcome aboard,' said Albert.

'Thanks. Can I call you Albert?'

'You sure can.'

The men's bags were stowed in the rear section of the vehicle and after locking up the premises the keys to the church and living quarters were deposited with a designated neighbour.

Albert drove the van on the first leg of its journey through the London suburbs and then through Kent towards the port of Dover.

An uneventful crossing on the ferry gave Albert the chance to rest up and when the ferry docked in Calais, Albert was still fresh enough to continue as the designated driver.

To make good time travelling south in France it had been decided to stick to the boredom of the French motorways. It meant missing out on the beautiful scenery of the French countryside but they had agreed that this wasn't a jolly boys outing and that rest and recuperation could happen after they achieved their goal. The motorway tolls would work out expensive but Aiden Doyle was paying for them.

Albert pressed on and was quite happy to press on as long as he felt fit to do so. Comfort stops were made at the motorway service areas and the three men made use of the toilet facilities in the rest areas. The opportunity to grab something to eat was taken and all bills were paid for by the Chancellor of the Exchequer, Albert.

Albert had calculated that a suitable stopping point would be in the Toulouse area not far from the Spanish border so when a Aires de Service showed up on the Satellite Navigation screen on the dashboard Albert plotted his way to that location. The Aires de Service were camping areas set up by the local council of the area to provide a stopping area for vehicles and passengers and were very popular with drivers of vehicles such as Albert's.

Albert pulled into the service area and noted that it was sparsely populated with vehicles. He parked the vehicle and Thomas connected it to the electrical supply.

The service area restaurant provided the men with a healthy meal although Albert noticed that Brendan only picked at his food. They retired for the night to their respective bunks in the cabin. Conversation was minimal. Albert drifted off to sleep after thinking about what lay ahead. Although their mission was deadly serious, he found the experience of working with these men towards a common goal quite exciting and reminded him of a joint venture he had been involved in times gone by.

49.

McMillan's hold on life was tenuous to say the least. He was lying badly injured on a ledge, below which was a sheer drop into a boulder-strewn ravine. He could not move because of his badly damaged shoulder and he could only prevent himself from falling by gripping onto a ridge of rock with his one good hand. He was petrified of falling asleep as this would have meant the loosening of his grip and he would almost certainly have plunged to his death below.

He had tried calling out for help but had given up as he seemed to be in the remotest place on the planet.

The one bit of good fortune that had befallen McMillan was that his prone position faced north so he was able to avoid the hot rays of the sun apart from the late afternoon. He was stung and bitten incessantly by insects but had to lie and suffer as any movement would have led to his downfall. He was parched beyond belief and thought about deliberately throwing himself off the cliff. Death would end his suffering.

He thought he was going to drift off into unconsciousness but somehow forced himself awake. He lay there listening for any sound but all he could hear were the insects chirping and buzzing around his face.

The darkness of the night dragged on interminably for McMillan and he struggled to keep awake.

After what had seemed an age the sun mercifully broke through to his right but he had just about had enough. He couldn't take much more of this.

He thought he heard a noise. He strained his ears. In the ravine below he could see an unkempt mongrel hound picking its way through the boulder strewn ravine. Thirty yards behind the dog a scruffy individual was carefully picking his way across the rocks and boulders and following the dog. The stranger called out to the dog.

McMillan shouted at the man for help but the man did not appear to hear him. McMillan shouted again. The dog started barking up at the ledge. On his third attempt at summoning help, the man looked upwards and, squinting through the sunlight, spotted McMillan cowering on the ridge. He indicated to McMillan to wait where he was. Although in pain and within minutes of being eaten alive McMillan found this to be somewhat amusing, wondering what else he was going to do other than stop on this ledge.

The man retraced his steps with the dog, now on a leash, and McMillan waited.

McMillan thought the man had forgotten about him, such was the time that had elapsed. McMillan consumed himself with thoughts of revenge on the person responsible for this. For the time being he had forgotten all about Albert Oxford. Little did he know that Albert Oxford hadn't forgotten about him!

A thick length of rope dropped over the cliff. It was knotted at the end. McMillan could hear voices at the top of the cliff edge. McMillan was unable to secure himself due to the extent of his injuries and indicated in his sufficient command of the language that he couldn't secure himself to the rope or use it to effect his escape from the ledge.

As McMillan clung for survival he heard scrambling from above. Small stones and pebbles dropped past him. A figure appeared above him. He was wearing the apparatus of an abseiler. He hung, suspended, beside McMillan and after manoeuvring along the ledge he was able to secure the other rope around McMillan's waist and under his armpits. On a given signal the rescue party at the top of the cliff started to pull McMillan upwards. The pain in his shoulder caused him to scream out in agony.

McMillan was hauled to the top and noticed the waiting ambulance. He was wheeled towards the ambulance doors on a trolley. Before being put in the vehicle the man who had initiated his rescue held out his hand. McMillan ignored the proffered hand.

50.

When Albert woke up he was disorientated. It took him a few seconds to realise he was lying on a bed in the motor home. The other two beds were unoccupied. Albert pulled on a pair of jeans and put on a t-shirt. The day was bright and already warm as he stepped outside the accommodation. He looked towards the restaurant area and spotted his two travelling companions sitting at a table near the window. He joined them and saw that Thomas was tucking into an omelette with sausages and bacon piled on the plate. Brendan was nursing a mug of coffee which smelt good.

Albert sat with them and ordered a coffee.

'What's the plan Albert?' asked Thomas.

'I've a contact in London, Thomas, and I'm going to use the burner phone to ask him to point us in the right direction.'

After breakfast and on his return to the cabin Albert sent a message to the holder of the other burner phone:

I need some help in locating the target.

After a wait of a few minutes, Albert received a reply on his phone with map coordinates accompanied by a message:

Our friend has been careless with the use of a credit card, paying for hotel stays of short duration. Otherwise he uses cash all the time.

Albert made a note of the hotel and then went to Google maps to explore the general location of their target. The area consisted of villages set below a Spanish mountain range north and inland of Valencia.

'I know where we're heading Thomas. We can expect to get there sometime this afternoon.'

I'll telephone our man in Spain and tell him where to meet us. I hope you'll be impressed with him Albert. He's a top man.'

'I'm sure I will, but what's in it for him? I know why you and I are doing it. And Brendan for that matter, but what's in it for your man?'

'You have to remember Albert, that we served together in the Middle East and other places. We saw things that were horrific. We stayed together, fought together and looked after each other's backs. Although he doesn't show it, Brendan is so looking forward to meeting up with our man.'

The motorhome with its three occupants drifted down to the Spanish border and crossed uneventfully and made its way to the province of Valencia. Albert steered the vehicle towards an Aire de Rest at the foothills of the mountains.

He chose their spot in the rest area, parked in the shade and connected the vehicle up to the electric supply. He noted that the Area was well served by a restaurant, shop and shower facilities.

Thomas made a phone call.

'Henry will be here early this evening. He'll join us for something to eat and to discuss the way forward.'

Albert was looking forward to meeting the man.

As they whiled the afternoon away by relaxing and talking Albert received a message on his burner phone. It was a grainy black and white photograph of a male person depicting just the head and shoulders. Below the photograph was a name: *Dennis C. McMillan.*

This was the first sight Albert had experienced of the man who had attempted to kill him on two occasions.

As the sun began its descent below the tip of the mountains the temperature cooled. The three men sat outside their motorhome at a plastic table. Brendan and Albert were drinking tea and Thomas drank from a bottle of Spanish beer.

In the distance Albert could hear the throaty roar of a motorbike.

Into the dusty arena of the Area de Rest the huge bike appeared. A large Harley-Davidson. It skidded to a stop a few yards away from the three men. The bike was placed on its stand by the colossus who had just dismounted.

Henry was at least six foot seven inches tall and was indeed a fine specimen of the male species. His long black hair reached his shoulders. He did not bother with wearing a cycle helmet. He was dressed in black denim jeans and wore only a black t-shirt that looked a couple of sizes too small due to the muscles and six-pack trying to burst out of confinement. On his upper arm a tattoo of a dagger and wings with the motto of the Special Air Service stood out.

Albert's two companions both moved forward to greet the man. The race was won by Brendan who bear-hugged the big man and didn't seem to want to let go of him. Albert sensed that Brendan was quite emotional and he eventually gave way to allow Thomas the opportunity to embrace his friend.

Albert was introduced to Henry who shook him warmly by the hand with a strong grip. A pack of beers was broken open.

The rest of the evening was spent in discussion. Albert summarised the position as he knew it. They were looking for Dennis McMillan who was known to work and live in the area not many miles away. He informed the group that McMillan was not living at the address registered to him and his work as a private investigator had come to a sudden halt.

Albert passed around the photograph of the man.

'Our first job obviously is to find him. Then we execute him and then we repatriate ourselves successfully,' said Albert.

'I agree that there's an urgency to finding him. My suggestion is that we get that photo copied and we then have to resort to old fashioned leg-work to track him down. I understand Albert that you've a supply of cash which can be used for persuasion, but I also believe in other forms of persuasion.'

Albert did not doubt that for one minute.

'I'm also in possession of a large amount of munitions which we can use if, and when, we need them,' Henry added.

It was agreed that the motorhome would be left where it was and would be used as a home base. Henry had the use of his motorbike and two other vehicles would be rented from a local car rental company. They would be utilised as runarounds.

Once the pack of Spanish beers had been demolished the men retired to their beds with Henry making use of the floor of the motorvan and covering himself with a blanket.

51.

Now that the Spanish hospital had confirmed that he had no broken bones and his shoulder had been strapped up, McMillan felt inclined to discharge himself. The hospital had rehydrated him and he was anxious to leave before the authorities came round asking awkward questions.

He phoned an Uber taxi and it took him back to his dingy motel. He checked his car and found it intact and free from vandalism. He took up occupancy of his room to sit and consider his options.

Top of the list was to take revenge on the people responsible for putting him in hospital after attempting to kill him.

In particular he wanted to hurt the slimy snake of a runt who ran the gang. El Poderoso. The toad was going to get a nasty shock.

McMillan also had another problem. He didn't like using credit or bank cards as they were traceable. He preferred to use cash whenever possible. On occasions it was unavoidable using plastic. He was running low on cash. He couldn't visit home because he was certain it was being watched. He missed his lady friend Carmela, but could not take a chance on seeing her or even contacting her. She was the daughter of El Caballo and he was now sure there had been some form of liaison between the two crime bosses.

Although he couldn't access his wall-safe in his office garage, he thought that he might be able to access the substantial garden of his property. So with this in mind he went to the dust covered car in the car park of the motel and drove carefully towards his home. His badly bruised shoulder made the journey painful but McMillan's determination was boosted by the thought of the game plan he was about to attempt to play.

McMillan sat in his car some distance away from the wall at the rear of his garden and waited until darkness had consumed the area. He left the vehicle and clambered over the brick wall. He knew the area like the back of his hand and crept to the spot that he sought.

With the spade from the boot of the car, he started to dig. It wasn't long before the sharp edge of the spade struck metal. McMillan carefully dug round the edges of the metal box and carefully prised it from the earth.

He retraced his steps back to the wall, hauling the box with his good arm. Once back over the wall the box was placed in the boot and covered with a blanket. McMillan drove back to his motel.

52.

After the four men had breakfast they sat round the table outside their motorhome. Brendan had made a supply of coffee. Albert had pored over a map of the area and had identified numerous villages near to where McMillan's credit card had last been used. Also factored into the equation were the villages in proximity to McMillan's home and work address.

Albert knew that McMillan had moored a motor boat in a small town marina. Enquiries would be conducted in the vicinity of the mooring.

It was decided that Brendan would be a pillion passenger on Henry's motorbike and would be dropped off to make enquiries in the villages. Henry would employ a similar strategy but working from the other end of the line of villages. They would meet up at the end of their day. Thomas and Albert would use one of the two hire cars to make enquiries at the marina.

They agreed that they would all meet up back at the motorhome after the day's work.

Albert's first task before they all set off was to accompany Henry on his motorcycle into the nearest big town where

Albert purchased four burner phones and accompanying sim cards.

Albert also found a 'print your holiday photos' shop and copied enough prints of the picture of McMillan. On his return Albert and Thomas set up the phones with the other numbers plumbed into the speed dial facility.

The phones were handed out. Each man was allocated a small package of Euros and each man was issued a photograph of Mcmillan.

The men set about their business for the day. Brendan gleefully sat on the rear pillion seat, thinking to himself how life had changed for the better in the last few days. He was looking forward to the adventure.

Albert and Thomas drove towards the seaside village in the hire car. The marina was busy with tourists strolling along the promenade. Seagulls swooped and swirled amongst the fishermen who had fishing rods protruding into the calm aquamarine water.

Albert spotted what he thought might be the office of the harbour master. He knocked on the door. The small stocky man looked at them quizzically. Albert produced the photograph and said to the man he was looking for his brother. The harbour master shrugged his shoulders but his attitude changed perceptibly when Albert produced a twenty euro note.

The harbour master allowed the merest trace of a smile to crease his face as he slipped the note into the top pocket of his shirt. He produced a clip board and pointed to the name of McMillan on the sheet. There was an address written below but Albert knew that McMillan was no longer at that address.

The man indicated the mooring berth of McMillan's craft and pointed in that direction. Thomas asked him if the boat had been used recently. The harbour master pointed to the log he was carrying. It showed that the boat had last been used some three weeks previously.

Thomas led the way to where McMillan's boat was moored. It bobbed in the water and looked unremarkable. There was nothing to help them here.

Albert's next port of call was to the address registered to McMillan. He had been informed by London that McMillan was no longer there but he wanted to visit the address just to make sure. He was interested in where McMillan worked and lived and he wanted to give the place a cursory glance.

A fifteen minute drive took the two men to McMillan's residence. The house was set in grounds that looked well tended. Set away from the main two-storey house was a large garage which had been secured with a lock and chain. Albert had presumed this to be McMillan's work space. Albert had noticed that there were no vehicles parked on the driveway.

Thomas crept round the back of the garage and noticed a closed window. As quietly as he could manage, he broke the glass with a small rock he had picked up from the gravel drive. The window lever allowed him to open the window and he climbed in.

Albert remained outside whilst Thomas gave the room a cursory glance. There was nothing obvious in the room that could be of assistance to them apart from confirming that McMillan was a private investigator. Absence of receipts showed a tendency to only deal in cash. This would make McMillan harder to trace.

The men retraced their steps and returned to their vehicle. Albert thought it would be prudent to stock up with supplies as would befit four grown men. A visit was paid to the supermercado.

Brendan had left the Area de Rest on the back of the Harley-Davidson being driven by Henry. Brendan couldn't believe how his life had changed in the last four days. He felt re-energised meeting up with two of his former military comrades. He felt as if he was being useful. He didn't know anything about the intended target apart from the fact that he had killed the priest, but if Thomas was so incensed about this killing then he would do anything to help.

Henry drove the huge bike to the village at the top of the mountain. Brendan would start his enquiries here and work his way down the mountain calling at each village and eventually meeting up with Henry who would start his enquiry at the village at the bottom of the village and work his way up to meet with Brendan.

Brendan's first port of call was a small town that featured many cafes and bars. At this particularly early time of day they were deserted save for a few barmen and waitresses cleaning tables and setting tables for lunch. Hopefully these would catch the eye of passing tourists.

Brendan sat down at one of the outside tables. His straw hat protected him from an already warm sun. As a stage prop he had purchased a Spanish newspaper which he pretended to read whilst waiting for the waitress to tend to him.

When she arrived Brendan ordered an Americano and produced the photograph of McMillan. In broken Spanish intermingled with English, he asked the young girl if she had seen the man, indicating to her that the man in the photograph was his brother who he was trying to establish contact with. She told him she hadn't, but took the photograph through to the bar area where she showed the photograph to the barman and an elderly lady who appeared to be chief sandwich maker and chef. Both shook their heads negatively. The chef returned the photograph to the waitress who then made apologies to Brendan.

At the other end of the mountain road Henry made an impression on the locals as he sat astride his Harley Davidson and pulled it back onto its stand. His tall frame unfurled itself and his black ponytail and large muscular frame set the local tongues wagging. Touches of silver had started to creep into his temples.

The village consisted of one main street. Henry approached a car repair garage and produced his copy of the photograph of McMillan. He received the first of many negative responses but he knew that this was going to be a long drawn out business. He took time out to refresh himself with coffee at one of the two street cafes.

Back at the Area de Rest, Albert and Thomas unpacked their provisions which had been purchased at the store. It was neatly stowed away.

Albert decided that he was going to show off his culinary

skills and set about preparing a dish of chicken and vegetables. Thomas made himself useful by peeling and chopping. Beers had been placed in the van's fridge and a table had been set up outside the van. Both men awaited the return of the Harley Davidson.

As the chicken dish and pans of vegetables simmered on the hot plates, Albert knocked off the top of a bottle of beer and sat with his foot up on another chair.

If it wasn't for the serious business of finding and executing McMillan he would have been very happy with his lot at that particular moment. A meal on the go in the kitchen area, a bottle of cold Spanish beer in his hand and the warm sunshine of this part of Spain heating his body. He was in the company of professional men who had the same objective as he had, albeit that he and Thomas had a bigger motive.

His thoughts were interrupted by the throaty roar of the returning motor bike. The bike swept into the dusty bowl of the parking area, sending up a cloud of dust to announce their arrival. The silver hair breaking through at Henry's temples was caught by the setting sun. Brendan was smiling and was sharing an anecdote with his hero as the bike was put onto its stand.

Albert had obviously passed the test as camp cook as the cleanliness of the plates indicated. Thomas opened some more bottles of beer and then commenced to clear away the dishes and cutlery. On his return Henry said to him,

'What colour would you like Thomas?'

'What do you mean?' replied Thomas

'Your waitress's apron that I'm going to buy you tomorrow?'

211

Henry ducked just in time to avoid the apple that had been hurled at his head.

After the laughter stopped, Albert addressed the group.

'How did things go today?'

We did one side of the mountain valley today. In all, six villages. We've another four to do tomorrow,' replied Brendan. 'How did you get on Albert?'

'The marina where he moored his boat didn't reveal anything. He hasn't used it for a few weeks. We paid a visit to his house and had a look in his garage which he uses as an office. He's not living at home.'

'It looks like he uses cash rather than plastic so this might take a bit of time,' added Thomas.

'Henry, I'd like you and Brendan to continue with your avenue of inquiry. I'm going to make a call to a source in London to see whether they've any updates for us.'

'And I presume Thomas is going to be making the beds and giving the place a bit of a clean-up,' laughed Henry.

Henry was not so adept at avoiding the bread roll thrown at him.

The beers were polished off.

53.

After a breakfast of toasted bacon sandwiches, prepared by Thomas, and washed down with coffee, the two men on the motorbike returned to the task of looking for a sighting of McMillan.

Brendan clung on to the back of Henry.

He idolised this man. Their joint enterprises in the deserts of the Middle East had bonded them into a formidable fighting duo. When their experience in Iraq came to a close they both left the unit. They drifted apart. Henry had emigrated to Spain where he kept himself active in garden construction and did the odd bit of work as a doorman for a company that specialises in supplying big ugly brutes to maintain the peace at clubs in his part of Spain. The one exception was that Henry was a handsome brute.

Brendan had drifted back to life in rural Bedfordshire staying with his sister. He couldn't keep down a job and had not realised that the effects of the Middle East war had left a profound effect on his mental stability. He had constant arguments with his sister resulting in Brendan moving out of his accommodation. He moved to London. He could not come to terms with the recommended hostel. He had taken to sleeping on park benches or shop doorways.

Purely by accident Thomas had happened upon him and had offered to help him. For a short time he used the hostel that Thomas resided at, but it was not long before Brendan returned to his favoured sleeping places in the open air.

Thomas kept an eye out for Brendan and would occasionally slip him some cash for a hot meal. When Brendan had been asked by Thomas to come on the trip he didn't express much enthusiasm until Thomas informed him that Henry was also coming to help them. That was the clincher for Brendan and he now found himself clutching on to his hero.

But the love, such as it was, was not all one-way traffic. Henry had been disappointed to hear of Brendan's lifestyle. The pair had been inseparable during their days with the unit. There was also the small matter that Henry owed his life to Brendan. During a shoot-out with the Mujahadeen, four of the group had retired to a hut built with sticks and mud. They had attempted to return fire but became entrapped in the hut. Four other members had retreated to the safety of a rocky ridge and dug in.

The mud hut came under rocket fire with one of the missiles destroying their cover in a cloud of sand and noise. Three of the four men in the hut ran for safety under heavy fire from the forces of Al Qaeda. The four SAS soldiers behind the ridge attempted to give covering fire but one of the men fleeing from the hut was seen to return to the decimated hut. His compatriots looked on in amazement whilst this lone figure re-emerged from the wreckage dragging a human form behind him.

With a great deal of bravery and fortune the soldier was able to drag the unconscious body to the safety of the ridge.

Thus it was that the diminutive Brendan Coleman saved the life of Henry Spearing. Thomas Cannon was one of the four men behind the ridge who gave covering fire.

Henry was eventually airlifted by helicopter to hospital after the enemy force had suffered losses from sustained fire and the planned use of their unit's top sniper. The SAS detachment with the seven remaining personnel intact, were able to retreat to a place of safety where they were scooped up by a Chinook.

Henry would be forever grateful to his friend and smiled to himself as he drove the pair of them to their assignment in the Spanish valley.

Albert walked to an area of the car park where the phone reception was marginally better. He spoke to his contact in London, who he presumed was Ted Fuller.

He updated him on the progress, or lack of it, and told him of his immediate plans. Thomas and himself would supplement the enquiries being made by Henry and Brendan.

'If we can't place him we might be struggling. He doesn't use credit cards or mobile phones. He's not living at home. There's no trace of his car. I'm wondering if he hasn't already been whacked by someone else. Either that or he's got wind of us looking for him and he's gone to ground.'

'I'll see what I can come up with,' said the voice on the other end. 'I'll ring you later this morning.'

Albert was tempted to thank Detective Sergeant Fuller but resisted and continued the pretence of not knowing who his informant was.

54.

McMillan put a pineapple in the right hand pocket of his linen jacket. In the interests of balance, and as a reserve, he placed another pineapple in the left hand pocket. He had taken the pineapples from his metal box. They fitted comfortably into the palm of his hand and were hewn from a bronze metal and were otherwise identified as M67 hand grenades complete with a pin that would be removed before causing mayhem and destruction. McMillan selected an automatic handgun to which he could fit a silencer attachment.

McMillan was desperate to seek revenge on the man who had attempted to kill him by instructing his thugs to throw him over the edge of a cliff.

He drove towards the village of Passina and parked his car in a shady copse of trees about a mile outside the village. He didn't stick to the road but walked a circuitous route that took him into the village through a collection of small holdings. Those working on the land tended to ignore the sole walker.

McMillan knew where El Poderoso held his council meetings and also knew that it would be the height of stupidity to approach the cafe entrance to the council headquarters occupied by Poderoso's gang.

McMillan had already decided to approach Poderoso's chambers from the rear. He kept a safe distance using trees and foliage as cover. He saw that the rear door to the premises was shut but McMillan knew that the target was inside the premises by the presence of one of the thugs leaning against one of the large industrial waste bins whilst acting as a sentry.

McMillan pulled up the bandana that he was wearing round his neck. He positioned it to cover his lower face and he pulled down his baseball cap tight onto his head. He approached the guard.

The large sentry spotted McMillan too late. McMillan shot him through the man's forehead with the minimum of noise. McMillan dragged the corpse behind the waste bins and approached the rear door. It was unlocked.

Brendan had been dropped off by Henry at the village at the lowest point of the steep valley. He would attempt to identify and locate McMillan and if unsuccessful he would take a local bus to the next village up the valley.

Henry had driven off up the mountain road to start at the topmost village. He had told Brendan he would meet up with him at one of the villages in the middle. When they had looked at the map of the valley they both agreed that the likeliest small town to meet would be that of Passina.

Brendan's routine and success rate had been similar to that of the previous day. He had been humoured, gaining sympathy from waitresses and bar staff. The local people felt sorry for this man looking for his brother.

After he had completed his tour of the first village Brendan decided that as the next port of call was a considerable climb, he would make use of the local bus service. He walked to the bus stop where he waited with the young mothers who had just picked up their children from the local nursery school that served that part of the area.

The conversation between mothers and their offspring was animated and exciting, as tales were told of pictures coloured and stories narrated by nursery assistants.

Brendan smiled at the infectious enthusiasm of the young children but noticed that as the local bus was approaching the village of Passina, the mood changed dramatically. The chatter which had been excitable was now moderated and conversations were reduced in tone. The smiles had disappeared.

As the bus pulled to a halt outside what appeared to be a library, Brendan noticed that this village differed to those he had already visited. The other villages had been sunlit, airy, whitewashed and had vibes of conviviality. This village was dark, in the shadow of the mountain, and had a foreboding menace exuding from its dark buildings.

Brendan walked down the only main street and chose to start at the cafe on the sidewalk sitting in the shade. It was difficult to tell if the cafe was open for business. The tables at the front on the raised pavement were unoccupied but Brendan thought he noticed movement behind the sunshades of the establishment.

He sat down and produced his usual stage prop in the form of a Spanish newspaper. Within a minute a grim-faced young waiter appeared and took his order of an Americano coffee.

Brendan pretended to read his day-old newspaper and sipped at his coffee. There was something that unnerved him about this small town. It just felt uncomfortable.

McMillan tested the door handle of the rear entrance to the restaurant. It opened without any noise. He entered and found himself in a utility room which contained two large fridges and two chest deep freezers.

McMillan listened at the door and could hear animated discussion. The participants were talking about their loss of control over drug supply and demand. One of the louder voices blamed the small rival gang led by El Caballo and beseeched his companions to wage war on their rivals.

McMillan tested the door to make sure it was unlocked. He ensured that his baseball cap was pulled tight onto his head and that his red bandana was covering the majority of his face.

He pulled the pin from the grenade, opened the door, and rolled the M67 pineapple across the floor in the direction of the six men sitting round a table in the plush restaurant. McMillan quickly closed the door and made good his escape through the outer door. Running at full pelt in the direction of his car, McMillan heard the explosion and thought to himself that it would be impossible for any of them to survive the blast.

El Poderoso saw the grenade bouncing across the parquet flooring in slow motion. He watched it, mesmerised.

One of his goons pushed him behind a low brick wall

separating the restaurant from the restrooms. The goon deliberately fell on top of him in an attempt to protect him. The explosion sent a cloud of debris, dust, furniture and potted flower plants cascading round the room. The noise was deafening.

When the dust settled a quietness had descended on the scene. The only noise was the quiet moaning of those injured. The gang chief had survived with minor cuts and abrasions. His ribs had been badly bruised by the man who had saved his life by falling on top of him. His saviour had bruises and cuts and shredded clothing, but was still alive.

Of the other four, two had obviously perished and the other two had survived but had life-threatening injuries. A lower limb belonging to one of the survivors lay on the opposite side of the room. The survivor was bleeding profusely. The saviour quickly applied a tourniquet fashioned from strips of torn tablecloths.

Outside the restaurant Brendan had been sitting quietly at his table when the noise of the explosion preceded the destruction of the front of the cafe area.

Brendan was showered by glass fragments as tables and chairs were knocked over by the force of the blast. He picked himself off the wooden flooring and was relieved to see that he had only suffered superficial cuts.

The cafe manager had also survived the explosion but now looked and surveyed Brendan with some suspicion.

Brendan asked him if there were other people in the rear of the restaurant. The man nodded. Brendan told him to ring the police and the ambulance service. The man took out his mobile and did as he was told.

Brendan walked through the cafe shop front and entered the restaurant area behind the bar. The smoke had cleared enough for him to survey a scene of devastation. At least two dead, two badly wounded and a big heavy topped individual sitting alongside a weasel of a man wearing a blue cashmere scarf. Weasel was on his mobile summoning the rest of his gang to attend the restaurant but when he saw Brendan he stopped. Both men looked at Brendan.

Quien eres tu

'Who are you?' asked the blue scarf.

Brendan indicated that he didn't understand the question. His minder produced a handgun and pointed it at Brendan. He indicated to Brendan to empty his pockets. Brendan took out a small amount of Euro notes, a mobile phone and the crumpled photograph of McMillan.

El Poderoso picked this up and looked at it with interest. A sneer crossed his face. He barked some instructions to the heavy who clumped Brendan on the side of his temple with the handgun. Brendan slumped unconscious to the dusty floor. The blow had caused his head to bleed profusely.

Poderoso's other gang members had wasted no time in getting to the restaurant in a variety of vehicles. One of the vehicles was a low flatbed truck with sides that could be dropped. The gang leader wanted the restaurant cleared of all casualties.

Two of the dead bodies were placed on the truck at the rear of the restaurant. The body of the sentry was also placed beside that of his two companion gang members. The two members who had been seriously injured were also manhandled onto the back of the lorry, as was the unconscious form of Brendan, who by now had his wrists secured with plastic cable-ties.

The 'scarf' instructed the driver to take the passengers to a building site to the north of the village. He imparted implicit directions as to what should take place.

El Poderoso was then driven by a young gang member to his apartment in the village overlooking the village square. He sat behind his oversized desk and telephoned El Caballo.

Henry rode the big bike slowly into the mountain village where he said he would meet Brendan. After fruitless enquiries in two villages he was looking forward to a cool drink whilst sitting in the shade of the tall trees that over-looked the cafe.

But something was not right. Apart from the fact that this village had a menacing feel to it, there was a lack of people and children bustling about the streets. Everybody seemed to be indoors. When he spotted the cafe he could see that the glass windows had been shattered and that the tables and chairs which had obviously been knocked over, were being picked up by the young waiter who looked agit-ated as he replaced the furniture into its rightful position.

Henry sat opposite on a wooden bench surveying the scene. There had obviously been some form of explosion and he was beginning to get worried for the safety of Brendan. He rang Brendan's burner mobile phone. There was no answer. He walked across the road to the cafe.

'I'm looking for my friend,' said Henry in his best Spanish. Henry described him. The young waiter shook his head.

'What has happened?' asked Henry.

'One of the electrical devices exploded,' he replied.

Henry pushed past him. The youth attempted to bar his way but Henry's size and power was a mismatch against the scrawny figure of the waiter. Henry entered what had been a plush restaurant but which was now reduced to rubble. Strewn curtaining on the floor could not conceal the blood which had started to congeal and dry. Particles of dust and brick had not fully settled and still floated in the air. The smell of cordite was noticeable.

Henry looked at the young man with a quizzical raise of his eyebrow.

'I cannot help you. Nobody can.'

'You will help me,' said Henry firmly and turned on his heel and walked out of the restaurant back to his Harley Davidson.

55.

Albert's burner phone rang. He could see that the call was coming from London.

'I've some information for you,' said the voice on the other end of the line.

'Go on,' said Albert.

'Your friend Peter who works in the Home Office, I used him to find out some information about the target McMillan.'

'Please tell, I'm all ears.'

'McMillan is a former police officer. Although he had to leave the Metropolitan Police before his official retirement date, he was still entitled to a police pension. Retired officers and those in receipt of a police pension are entitled to receive it anywhere in the world. McMillan has instructed Police Pensions to transfer his money to an account in Spain. McMillan has chosen an Oficina de Correos, which is a Post Office to you. It is paid into that Office on a certain date each month and McMillan withdraws the full amount in Euros. He doesn't always withdraw it on the actual day but usually picks it up within three days at most.'

The London caller then told Albert the date of the receipt of pension. Albert noted that the day in question was the following day. Albert was also informed of the village that housed the Oficina de Correos.

Albert imparted his news to Thomas. Thomas looked pleased with the information and the pair of them decided to have a run in the car to the village to familiarise themselves with the location and to look for any potential problems.

Henry sat astride his Harley Davidson at the end of the village street. He had tucked himself behind a hedge of purple bougainvillea but he maintained clear vision on the front door of the cafe.

Customer footfall was non-existent. The only sign of life was a handyman who turned up with his bag of tools and proceeded to repair the front of the shop with plyboard affixed to the window frame. A crude notice indicating that the cafe was still open for business was scrawled across the plyboard.

The waiter that Henry had spoken to previously picked up the chairs that had fallen over and swept the boardwalk outside the cafe.

Henry continued his vigil and took aboard sustenance in the form of a banana and bottled water.

The brightness of the day and accompanying heat slowly gave way to dusk and a welcoming drop in temperature. Henry's attention was drawn to the cafe manager locking the front door to the premises. He had wheeled out a push bike from inside the cafe. He mounted the bike and began to ride up the hill leading out of the village.

Henry followed on his own transport from a respectable distance, conscious of the fact that his motorbike had a growl that could be heard some distance away.

The youth was struggling to cycle up the hill but on reaching a crossroads he took a turn that led him down a grassy path. Henry didn't take any chances and dismounted his bike. He tucked it away into the dense foliage so that it was unseen from the path. He had to expend some energy by running after the cyclist on foot but thankfully the cyclist seemed to be relaxed and he took his time to reach a small brick white-washed building set in a copse of trees. Two small boys ran out to greet him. He ruffled their hair and handed each of them a fruit bar.

Henry watched the man and the two small boys enter the house by the front door of the single storey house. He circled round to the rear of the house being careful to use the trees as cover. At the rear of the house was a small vegetable garden which had been carefully tended. A washing line was strung across the space just outside the rear door. A couple of hens pecked at the ground near the vegetable patch.

A lithe young woman emerged from the rear door and persuaded the hens to enter the chicken coop where they would be safe through the night from any prowling beasts. She was dressed in a white blouse and knee length skirt. It looked to Henry that another child was imminent. Henry was slightly envious of what appeared to be an idyllic lifestyle but these thoughts did not last long when he remembered that this youth had said he was unable to help him.

Henry bided his time and sat on a grassy clump. He could see the rear door and noted that the property had an outside toilet. He was pretty certain that this would be the only room of convenience that the house possessed.

After a wait of about an hour, Henry saw the light from inside the house open up onto the darkness of the back garden area. The waiter emerged and entered the outhouse to relieve himself. Once finished he opened the toilet door to return to the comfort of his family.

Suddenly, and without any sort of warning, he was grabbed from behind by a pair of arms that were so powerful he was rendered incapable of resisting. A giant hand was clamped over his mouth and he was dragged and lifted into the trees some hundred yards from the house.

Henry was able to speak rough Spanish due to the amount of time he had spent in Spain. The waiter had picked up a good smattering of English due to serving English and American tourists who had stopped at his cafe on their way to more luxurious places.

'What's your name?' asked Henry

The youth was shaking visibly

'Edouardo,' replied the man.

'You told me earlier that you would not be able to help me,' growled Henry

'Yes.'

'And I told you that you would help me. Okay?'

'Yes,' squeaked Edourardo.

'Well, here is the deal Eddie,' said the big man

'It's Edouardo,' said the Spaniard.

He received a sharp crack across his face from the back

of Henry's right hand.

'Well Eddie, here is the deal. You're going to tell me what has taken place today. If I think you are telling me the truth I may allow you to live to see your sons' next birthdays. If I don't believe you, you'll perish by my fair hands and I'll then have the difficult choice of who I kill after you. What do you think? Your wife, followed by both of your boys? Or the other way round?

Edouardo started to shake and whispered,

'Please, no.'

Spoken with menace Henry Armstrong said 'My friend, the choice is in your hands. Take your time and tell me everything.'

Edouardo started to tell Henry Spearing everything. El Poderoso was an evil man who controlled not only his own village, but those dotted along the sides of the valley. He ran a drugs operation whereby the drugs were imported illegally from North Africa. He ruled with a fist of iron and lived in a fourth-floor de-luxe apartment overlooking the town square of Passina.

Nothing in the area was done without his permission. The local Mayor was under his control and did everything he was asked to do. At the moment there had been a problem importing the drugs as someone in the operation had gone rogue.

There was a rival gang in the next valley along the mountain range run by a man called El Caballo. He operated out of a village called Tajeda. El Poderoso allows him to run his own little operation provided he does not interfere in Poderoso's enterprises.

'What happened today?' asked Henry.

'I run the cafe. At the back of the cafe is a really smart restaurant. Poderoso uses this restaurant as his council headquarters. When they were in there today there was an explosion. Two of his men got killed. They found another dead gang member at the back door. He had been guarding the rear of the restaurant. Two other members of his gang were badly injured. El Poderoso just had cuts and bruises.'

'That's a shame,' said Henry. 'I want to ask you about a friend of mine.'

'He was sitting outside the cafe having a coffee when the explosion happened. He had asked me about his brother and showed me a photograph of him. Two of Poderosos gang came and grabbed him.'

'What happened to him?'

'He was taken out the back and placed in the back of the truck with the dead men and the two injured men.'

'Where did they go?'

'I don't know.'

'You were doing so well, Ed. I don't want you to spoil things for yourself or your family. Think carefully and tell me,' said Henry.

Edouardo hesitated.

'I'm waiting,' said Henry, 'but not for much longer.'

'He has a building site just outside the village. He's building cheap housing. He hasn't got planning permission but he has the local Mayor and the Spanish Guardia all in his pocket. If you drive north you won't miss it because he has a couple of those huge cranes putting it all together cheaply.'

'Where else could they be?' asked Henry.

'You won't like this,' answered the Spaniard.

'Try me,' said Henry Spearing.

Edouardo looked him in the eyes.

'He has a pig farm two kilometres further up the road. The animals are huge. It is said that all dead people are fed to them.'

Edouardo hesitated again and Henry had a premonition about what he was going to say next.

'Not just dead men, but also ones who are alive and who have upset him.'

Henry's worst fear had been confirmed.

'How will I find the farm?'

'You will be able to smell it.'

'This is the situation my Spanish friend.' Henry put an arm around Edouardo's shoulder. Edouardo was apprehensive as to what was going to happen next. He shivered. He glanced towards the small house that contained his wife and two young sons.

'You won't breathe a word of our little meeting to anyone. Not even your wife. If you do, your family will be fed to the pigs. Do you understand me?'

Edouardo shuddered but nodded his head.

'Now, off you trot and be a good boy.'

Henry watched as Edouardo scampered back down the incline to the safety of his family home.

56.

Albert and Thomas had found the Spanish Post Office fairly easily. It sat in the middle of a row of shops and business premises. The Correos had as its neighbours a small Spanish estate agent which had a window full of holiday lets. The shop on the other side of the Correos was a fruit and vegetable outlet with an impressive arrangement of fresh fruit and vegetables neatly stacked in pyramids in an attractive display.

While Thomas stayed with the car, Albert sauntered over to the estate agent's premises and pretended to be interested in looking at the villas and apartments for sale or for letting. Albert remembered fondly his apartment in Spain before he had been tracked down by the Metropolitan Police in time gone past.

He glanced at the photographs but was more interested in the layout of the Post Office. The window was full of advertisements for postal services and just like the UK he noticed a cork board full up with handwritten adverts for gardeners and cleaners.

There was only one entry door and it led to the counter at the back of the office. This counter had a protective screen. Albert saw an orderly queue waiting to be served by the one employee, an old lady with grey hair who was sitting and smiling at customers who appeared to be regulars.

Albert knew that he was at least a day early but was satisfied that this shop did not present a problem as far as observation was concerned. Almost opposite was a street cafe selling bocadillos and coffee. There was seating and tables outside the cafe and Albert could see that there was similar furniture inside the premises.

Both men were pleased with their reconnaissance and drove back to the Area de Rest. After opening up the motorhome, Thomas pulled down the awning and set out a table and chairs in the shade. Albert opened a couple of beers.

'Have you thought about a plan Albert. What are you going to do?' asked Thomas.

'Not really, Thomas,I think it'd be better if we tail him from the post office and execute him away from the gaze of the locals. But no, I just want to end him.'

'Amen to that,' said Thomas.

As the two men sat sipping from their respective bottles a cloud of dust and noise preceded the entrance of the Harley Davidson which slid to a halt next to them.

Henry never wore a crash helmet when riding his machine and both men could see that Henry was in an agitated state as he hauled the bike back onto its stand.

'Boys, we have a major problem,' exclaimed the giant man.

Henry told the two men what had happened earlier and

how he had put pressure on Edouardo in an effort to pin-point where Brendan might be.

Both Thomas and Albert were concerned and looked at Henry for inspiration.

'What do we do next?' asked Albert.

'How can you be sure that this waiter will not spill the beans?' asked Thomas.

'I'm as sure as I can be that he won't,' replied Henry, 'but this runt of a gang boss has huge influence and his tentacles stretch far and wide. We can't trust anyone but as far as Edouardo is concerned he won't want his family fed to the pigs on El Poderoso's pig farm. That should be one of the places we focus on but we may also have to look at a building site where he is building the cheap rental apartments. We also have to make sure that there is no trace of Brendan at the cafe that was blown up. I'm fairly sure that he's not there as Edouardo would've told me.'

'I'll cover the Post Office on my own tomorrow. If I spot McMillan I'll try to tail him without showing out. But your priority is to locate and get Brendan back here.'

'We're agreed on that Albert,' said Henry, 'but don't take any chances with McMillan. I suspect that it's him who blew up the cafe. I don't know why, but he's proved he's dangerous. He's upset two crime bosses and their gangs already so he won't think twice about trying to take you out. I just hope it isn't third time lucky.'

'Thanks for that vote of confidence, Henry.'

It was agreed that Henry would take his motorbike and Thomas would take one of the cars. Albert would remain at base camp and monitor phone calls on the burners.

The men fist-bumped before Henry and Thomas drove off in their respective vehicles.

Albert watched them depart and finished off his beer. He thought about what lay ahead of the three of them, not knowing that the following forty eight hours would be pivotal for the rest of their respective lives.

Henry had asked Thomas to follow him on his huge bike. After travelling several miles, Henry drove through a small village and pulled into a cul-de-sac that housed a set of lock-up garages. Henry unlocked one and switched on the interior light.

Thomas couldn't believe his eyes. The garage was a veritable munitions store containing everything that would assist in invading a foreign country. Or so it seemed.

Henry picked up the supplies he thought he would need. He tossed a Kevlar bullet proof sleeveless vest to Thomas. Thomas slipped on the vest. He knew from experience that the vests provided high impact resistance, They were strong and lightweight.

Henry picked up two Heckler and Koch MP5K submachine guns with ammunition clips. He tossed a black balaclava to Thomas and a pair of black nylon gloves with a reinforced palm grip. A tin of blackening agent was placed next to the weapon and ammunition.

Henry added four stun grenades to the canvas bag he had selected.

'Does it take you back to the day, Thomas?'

'It sure does mate. I just hope we'll have the same success rate.'

Thomas tempered his thoughts by remembering that not

every operation was a success. They had left many good friends behind in the sandy deserts of Iraq and the rolling green hills of Antrim.

They both travelled in the car with Thomas driving and Henry charting their route to where he thought the pig farm was situated, Thomas hoped that they wouldn't chance across meeting any enforcement officers en route. What would they make of the two of them all dressed up to rescue Brendan and assassinate the opposition?

Henry's first port of call was to the pig farm. He had a rough idea where it was if Edouardo was to be believed.

Sure enough the devastating smell of pig manure crept into the car. Thomas pulled over into a copse of trees and both men set off on foot, armed to the teeth, to cover the 800 yards that lay between them and the outbuilding that oversaw about twenty pens of pigs. At this time of night the animals were safely in their pigsties.

While Thomas waited at the end of the grassy path leading to the outhouse, Henry crawled towards the window and peered in through the curtainless window. A low light showed an elderly man asleep on a makeshift bed made up of an old mattress. Henry assumed that he was the only person present and returned to Thomas.

'Just an old man sleeping. Brendan isn't there. We'll move on to the building site.'

Brendan had regained consciousness. His whole body hurt. He had been struck a violent blow on his head and the journey in the back of the truck had been uncomfortable and painful.

The blindfold had been removed and he tried to gain a

sense of where he was. He was in an office of some description. He could see a makeshift table with charts and building plans strewn over it. It had the appearance of being a cabin. As he lay on the dirty dusty floor he could hear two gravelly voices speaking behind him. Lying prostrate he attempted to turn around so that he could get a look at his captors. He received a kick in the ribcage for his troubles.

The two Spanish gang members finished speaking. One of them lifted Brendan onto a rickety wooden chair. The blindfold was placed back over his eyes.

One of the Spaniards spoke passable English.

'We want to know why you were trying to trace the man in the photo.'

Brendan did not reply.

'You will need to tell us. If you do not tell us we will take you to the farm where you will be fed to hungry pigs. Now, what have you got to say?'

'Any chance of a cup of tea? Milk, no sugar, please.'

Brendan received a crack across the face. He had expected this and rode the blow. He smiled in the direction of where he guessed his assailant stood.

Another blow struck him on the side of the head. This caused him to fall to the floor of the cabin. He was forcibly dragged up off the floor and placed back on the wooden seat.

The two dark shapes approached the building site cabin stealthily. Henry saw that there was a light on, barely illuminating the inside of the structure.

As Thomas waited some 20 yards away, Henry crawled on all fours to the base of the window. He slowly lifted himself and peered through the dirty window pane. He saw Brendan sitting on a wooden chair. His hands had been tied behind his back and he had been blindfolded with a dirty rag. Henry could see a streak of dried blood which crossed Brendan's face. Henry signalled for Thomas to join him.

The Spaniard leant in close to Brendan's face. Brendan could feel his hot breath.

'Senor, this is your last chance to tell me why you are looking for the man in the photograph. He has killed three of my friends and unless you tell me the reason you are looking for him I will have to kill you.'

The Spaniard pressed the muzzle into Brendan's cheekbone.

Leaning close to Brendan he said,

'This is your last chance to tell me what I want to know. This could be your last chance to speak to me.'

Brendan leant his head towards the Spaniard and said,

'Your breath stinks.'

The Spaniard pulled the trigger and shot Brendan through his cheekbone just as two men dressed in dark clothing and wearing balaclavas crashed through the flimsy office door.

They fired their automatic weapons. Henry pumped a burst into the assassin whilst Thomas took out the other gang member with one shot into his neck.

Both men died instantly. Thomas felt for a pulse in both men. None existed. Henry went to Brendan and cradled his head in his arms but there was nothing he could do for his colleague and friend.

Thomas collected the car whilst Henry gathered up some workmens' tools and a length of canvas tarpaulin.

Before leaving the building site both men removed their balaclavas and gloves. Thomas placed them in an empty oil can which had been used for rubbish. Thomas set it alight with accelerant.

The body of Brendan was laid on the rear seat and the tools placed in the boot. The two men were shocked beyond belief and nothing was said. Henry knew what they had to do and drove quietly towards the coast.

When Henry reached a suitable spot he stopped the car. They were at the top of a hill which had a view down to the sea. The sunrise was some three hours away but the ripples on the moonlit sea could be spotted from their vantage point. Henry tossed a spade to Thomas and with both men toiling for over two hours they had managed to dig a suitable resting place for their friend.

Both men lifted Brendan's corpse and placed it in the canvas tarpaulin. It was crudely fastened with string and the body bag was carefully placed at the bottom of the grave. The hole in the ground was filled in by both men. Thomas made an elementary cairn from rocks lying in the scrub. Henry placed his arm round Thomas's shoulders.

As the men stood in silence the sun's first yellow edge started to appear above the eastern horizon. Brendan was not the first colleague they had buried on foreign soil but this was the most personal. The others had been buried in the sands of the Middle East although some had been repatriated in a bodybag to the United Kingdom via RAF Brize Norton.

Both men bowed their heads for a last time before getting back into the car. The drive back to see Albert was made in silence. As they entered the Area de Rest, Albert was sitting outside the motorhome under an awning drinking from a mug of freshly brewed coffee. When the two men got out of the car he could see instantly that something was badly amiss.

Albert was shocked after hearing their news.

'He had a death wish,' said Thomas. 'He felt his life was not worth living but he'd been given this last opportunity to meet up with Henry and to contribute to something useful.'

The news was indeed truly terrible. Although he had not known Brendan for long, the manner of his death was shocking and Albert felt for his two companions who had campaigned with their late friend. Henry was particularly upset. He remained silent over coffee. Thomas said,

'Brendan has had a shit few years and in the last few days I've never seen him happier. He knew of the danger involved with this venture and was probably quite happy that it ended this way, if you know what I mean?'

Henry nodded in agreement.

'He was a loyal colleague. I owe him and I will never forget him.'

'We've a divergence here,' said Albert. 'I can understand if the pair of you want to exact vengeance on the person responsible. I don't have a problem with that. I can busy myself by looking for McMillan and identifying where he is holed up. The pair of you can do what you like but be careful. We've just lost a good friend and I don't want to lose any more.'

Henry looked pensive, rubbing the stubble on his chin.

'You two concentrate on McMillan. That's why you came here. I will take care of the other thing.'

Albert looked at Thomas who just nodded in agreement.

'Someone is going to get a slap,' said Henry, 'and I'll need a lift back to pick up my bike and to get rid of the arsenal we've got in the car.'

Whilst Henry showered and removed the blackening from his face Albert asked Thomas,

'What did Henry mean by giving someone a slap?'

Thomas smiled.

'Don't even think about it Albert. We'll probably read about it in the newspapers or see it on television.'

A frown creased Albert's forehead. He didn't want the actions of Henry Spearing, whatever they were, to affect his pursuit and assassination of McMillan. He did, however, appreciate the murderous intent lodged in Henry's mind and the reason for it.

As Thomas drove off with Henry, Albert prepared himself for his day of observation watching the Spanish Correos, hoping to catch a sighting of the man responsible for the death of Michael Creaney and for the attempt on his own life.

57.

ennis McMillan sat in his uncomfortable motel room. The heat was stifling and the rickety fan provided by the seedy receptionist was too noisy to allow sleep. McMillan thought about his situation.

He was running short of cash, his sole method of purchase, and missed his girlfriend Carmela and in particular the services she provided. His private investigator's business was virtually non-existent now due to not being serviced by himself. He had killed his assistant who had managed to keep it afloat on days where he had been up to no good in the UK.

The lack of any news about El Poderoso had made him think that the gang boss had survived the grenade attack. That wouldn't be the end of the matter. The little weasel had attempted to kill him. He had to work out a plan to get back at him.

Contact from London had come to a stop but he couldn't think about that at the moment. Albert Oxford was the furthest thing from his mind. Once he had disposed of El Poderoso he could re-focus on Oxford. The retainer being paid by the Edmonton detective would be handy and was fairly lucrative.

Today he would make the drive to the Spanish Post Office to pick up his pension. He was able to withdraw it in cash which suited his purposes.

Albert parked his car behind the cafe. He walked up a side alley and sat at one of the plastic covered tables. He ordered a coffee from the young waitress and placed his copy of El Pais on the table and pretended he could read the printed words in the newspaper.

He had picked a table in the shade but had a clear view of the street door of the Post Office. The town was not busy. Parents were returning on foot, having dropped their offspring at the town school.

The Post Office had a steady trickle of customers and the estate agents next door did not attract anyone. Maybe too early in the day for prospective buyers or lettors.

After a couple of hours Albert felt it was time to order a ham and cheese sandwich and a cerveza. No sooner had this order arrived at his table when he felt a tap on his shoulder. He hadn't heard the man approach. He instantly recognised him.

'Fancy seeing you here,' said the man.

58.

The head of the rival gang, El Caballo, had held a meeting of his troops in the disused nightclub in the middle of the main street. The dilapidated building was literally falling apart but served a useful purpose for El Caballo and his troops. It also suited their scruffy demeanour. El Caballo's gang were allowed to operate by the ogre, El Poderoso, as they didn't pose a threat at the other end of the next valley. But, things had changed.

Word had gotten round that the rival gang had suffered multiple fatalities, including the drug runner who collected the consignments from the depths of the Mediterranean. Other fatalities had included a few of El Poderoso's closest henchmen. Their headquarters had been bombed and El Caballo was now trying to impress upon his men that maybe the time had arrived for his crew to take over operations.

It would mean a swift and decisive strike against the other mob but there was a fly in the ointment in the form of a vigilante riding his giant steed on two wheels. He had been causing mayhem in the next valley and, as he was a loose cannon, his team would have to be careful.

In an ideal world they would have to take him out first before moving on to El Poderoso.

His passionate hate of Dennis McMillan, who had deflowered and sullied his beautiful daughter Carmela, could be put on hold as they had heard that a small team of foreigners were tracking McMillan. In that respect he told his listeners that this would have to be handled with extreme care as the tracking team might easily be working with the local police or other authorities.

He summarised by saying that the first priority would be to track and eliminate the giant on the big motorbike.

Henry Spearing had decided that he would carry out some casual surveillance on the whereabouts of the man ultimately responsible for the death of his friend Brendan.

He parked his bike well outside the village of Passina. It was tucked behind a clump of scrub well off the beaten track.

Most of the narrow roads in the village ran into the town square which was the focal point for the inhabitants. The square boasted three small restaurants, a clutch of estate agents and a host of shops with fresh pyramids of fruit and vegetables neatly displayed. These shops were supplemented by a butcher's shop and a fresh fish shop, both of which displayed fresh clean produce.

An idyllic small Spanish town, Henry thought, apart from the fact that there was an absence of joy or happiness. There was no laughter from the young children and the adult population seemed to permanently wear expressions of sadness and gloom.

Henry realised that the cause of this depression was the

figure who controlled their lives. His fourth storey apartment was set in a red brick building and overlooked the square.

Henry noted the presence of a goon sitting in a black saloon car outside the main double doors of the entrance to the apartments. The windows of the vehicle were tinted black and the driver, or bodyguard, sat in the driver's seat with the air conditioning operating and a music tape playing Latin American dance music.

Henry presumed that there would be other guards outside the door of the apartment of El Poderoso. He decided that he would spend a bit of time sitting at one of the cafes and ordered a cool drink.

After thirty minutes Henry saw the driver of the tinted car sit up and adjust the seat position of the driver's seat. Sure enough, the runt, with his trademark cashmere blue scarf walked up to the rear door of the saloon car. A heavy who had followed him out, opened the door for his boss and got into the other rear seat. The car drove off in a flurry of dust.

Henry walked round the square attempting to keep a low profile and opened one of the double doors to the apartments.

Facing him was an expansive foyer with large plants dotted round the edges of a marble floor. Four expensive comfortable settees formed a square in the middle of the floor. A large low oak table was placed in the middle of the settees. Opposite the entrance doors was a reception desk which was manned by a young muscular Spaniard.

'Do you have any spare rooms?' asked Henry using his

best Spanish.

'No, Senor, these are private apartments.'

'Oh, I'm sorry, it looks like a hotel.'

'It used to be, but not any more.'

Thanking the receptionist, Henry took his leave. He made his way around the back of the apartment block. He spotted a rear door for service deliveries and where residents could dispose of their household rubbish into two large rubbish containers. An obligatory goon was slumped on a plastic chair looking at his mobile phone. Henry made sure he didn't get spotted.

Henry Spearing was still operating at fever pitch over the death of his companion but vowed that he needed to make a calculated measured response to negate this gang leader.

He had been prepared to do it alone but reluctantly realised that he would have to enlist the help of Thomas Cannon, a man with whom he had worked successfully with in the past and who he could trust with his life. He rang Thomas on his burner phone.

59.

Albert had frozen when the hand had been placed on his shoulder. As he turned round to look at the owner of the hand, the man's mobile phone rang.

'Henry, how can I help you?'

Albert let out a sigh of relief. It could easily have been the figure of McMillan who had crept up on him in an unguarded moment. He smiled in relief at seeing that it was the big frame of Thomas.

After Thomas had finished speaking to Henry he updated Albert.

'Henry wants me to give him a leg-up with the assassination of El Poderoso,' said Thomas, matter-of-factly.

'Is he going to get a slap?' Albert smiled.

He told Thomas that as it was late in the day, the chances of McMillan appearing at the Post Office was now minimal and he encouraged Thomas to meet up with Henry. Thomas departed the scene.

Albert was about to call his own surveillance to a halt as the temptation of a cold beer back at the mobile home was too tempting to resist.

A dark saloon crept into view from his left hand side and

parked outside the Post Office. Out of the driver's seat stepped the unmistakable figure of McMillan. He looked a bit haggard and appeared as if he had been sleeping rough. He went into the Correos, presumably to collect his pension.

Albert hurriedly retrieved his hire car and drove to a position a hundred yards behind McMillan's car and facing in the same direction.

Albert cursed his luck. He could have used the services of either Thomas and his car, or Henry and his Harley Davidson, or even both, as the effort of trying to tail a target single handedly was fraught with the danger of being spotted in the target's rear-view mirror.

McMillan did not spend long in the Post Office and returned to his vehicle and moved away from the kerb. Albert's luck was already at a stretching point when McMillan performed a U-turn and drove back past Albert who quickly ducked down into his seat.

Not a great start! Albert took his time and performed a similar U-turn, but only when he thought it was safe to do so without attracting the attention of the target.

Albert had a problem. He had to maintain a distance between himself and McMillan but he didn't want to lose the car in front. He didn't want to be compromised and abandon the surveillance as the next time McMillan would call at the Post Office would be in four weeks' time.

Albert had always smiled at the old films on television where the suspect would be followed by a car directly behind the target car. If only it was that easy!

McMillan drove for about ten kilometres driving through a couple of small towns. These towns afforded

Albert the luxury of putting another vehicle between himself and McMillan. Thankfully progress would not be obstructed by the interference of traffic lights.

About 200 metres ahead Albert saw the SEAT pull into the car park of a run-down motel. McMillan parked his car under the shade of a tree, locked the car, and went into the motel through the rear car park door.

Albert was fairly confident that he had housed McMillan and could take a bit more time in having to deal with him.

He gave it some thought and he figured that the best time to strike would be in the small hours of the morning and that around 4am was perfect. That would allow him enough time to get some rest and prepare himself in order to execute his plan and his target.

Albert returned to the motorhome and showered. He laid out his black assault gear, his Glock handgun and ammunition clip. All supplied by his own munitions armourer, Henry Spearing. He climbed onto his mattress. He set his watch alarm for 3am.

Albert couldn't sleep. His mind kept drifting as to how far he had come in the last few weeks.

He had survived an assassination attempt on his life by the man now holed up in the motel. Albert had found happiness living under the shelter of Father Michael Creaney. Although Creaney was a man of God, it had not prevented the pair of them being the best of friends. He had never been happier than the time spent living and working at St Paul's Church. He had made friends with Thomas Cannon and was attempting to make inroads into forming a friendship with the house-keeper, Helen. Albert had been smitten by the lady's charm and gentleness. It was a bonus that she was extremely attractive. Albert felt a pang of sorrow and regret that he would probably never see her again.

This had been caused in no small part by the activities of Dennis McMillan who had brutally murdered the priest. Albert had vowed he would avenge the death of Michael Creaney and was thankful that he was assisted by Thomas Cannon and Henry Spearing.

Albert thought about Brendan, another casualty of this venture. He had been deeply saddened by his death and now considered his own involvement in his death. Albert recalled that he had either been directly or indirectly involved in the deaths of numerous people who he had been in contact with.

Sleep did not come easy but eventually Albert drifted off into slumber only for his peacefulness to be awoken sharply by the sound of his watch alarm going off at 3am.

Henry Spearing and Thomas Cannon discussed the plan they intended to put into operation. Henry wanted Thomas with him in order that he could utilise his driving skills and experience in order to further their plan. Henry dropped Thomas at the building site with express instructions as to what he had to do.

Meanwhile, Henry parked his transport and walked towards the village of Passina. He stuck to the shadows. The last of the bars and drinking venues had closed and the local inhabitants had retired to their houses and apartments. Henry headed for the apartment block where he hoped he would find El Poderoso.

60.

Thomas could see a low light in the building site cabin. He guessed that the night watchman would be asleep. He crept carefully to the grimy window and was able to see that the security man was indeed asleep in a chair. Thomas tested the door to the cabin and found that it was unlocked. Very carefully, he slowly opened the door.

Unfortunately it creaked as it was opened and the guard woke with a start. Before he could move he was rendered unconscious with a shuddering blow to his head with the heavy duty torch that Thomas was carrying. He was expertly trussed up with gaffa tape taken from Thomas's work bag.

He had a quick look round the cabin and spotted what he was looking for. A set of keys hanging on a hook just by the door. Thomas took these and left the cabin and walked towards the vehicle that Henry had pinpointed and had requested.

Thomas's career in the various army postings had involved transportation and he had driven most forms of transport, but this task would be a first for him.

Henry took up his surveillance position at the rear of the

block of apartments. He thought that entry via the main street door would be too obvious and he ran the risk of being compromised.

His position overlooked the rear entrance to the block and included an area of large refuse bins which were serviced on a weekly basis. Henry noted that the bins had obviously just been emptied but that they still retained a stench of rotten fruit and vegetables.

Henry also noted the presence of a guard. He was dressed casually in denim jeans and a black leather jacket. Henry presumed that he would be armed. Henry crept up to within five yards of the guard. Henry shot the guard through the carotid artery on his neck with the handgun he had selected for this purpose and which had been fitted with a silencer attachment.

The guard had died instantaneously. Henry was able to lift him into one of the refuse bins where his body clunked onto the floor of the bin.

Henry Spearing moved silently into the main body of the apartment block. Using the rear service stairs, Henry emerged onto the fourth floor and carefully looked down the parquet flooring of the hallway. Another goon was sitting outside the large wooden oak door.

He was reading a magazine but not for much longer. Before he could react Henry had clubbed him unconscious and he fell to the floor in a heap.

Unfortunately, the noise had disturbed the occupant of the apartment. Henry flattened himself against the wall. The door was opened by the crime-lord. He saw the crumpled body of his guard lying on the floor but before he could close the door Henry had gripped him round his scarred neck with a vice-like grip.

El Poderoso was punched to the floor and lay there trembling. The body of the guard was dragged inside the apartment. Henry rendered the guard incapable of movement with liberal use of the tape. He also used tape to secure the hands of the crime boss and placed a gag across his mouth. This was also secured by tape.

Henry looked at the pathetic wretch snivelling and crying before him. He could only have weighed 8 stone wringing wet. He was dressed in a white nightshirt which he wore over a pair of boxer shorts. His spindly hairy legs protruded below the night shirt. To think that this creature controlled the lives of hundreds of people and made their lives a misery amazed Henry.

'You're a fucking embarrassment pal. Look at you. You're fucking pathetic.'

El Poderoso could not, or did not want to understand what had just been said.

'Payback time mate.'

Henry sat with the gang boss awaiting the call from his team mate Thomas. It was 4am and darkness still pervaded the small town.

Thomas had never driven one of these machines before. The controls were alien to him. He climbed up into the cab of the vehicle and examined what was in front of him. He spotted the empty ignition slot and placed the ignition key into the dashboard. He turned the key and an engine spluttered into life.

He had a gear console in front of him. He figured which

gears were forward gears and guessed that one of the gear positions would enable him to reverse the vehicle.

The method of travel would be slow and laborious as the vehicle was set on track wheels.

Another gear console sat to his right hand side. This collection of gears operated the machinery which sat above his head. Thomas flicked on a switch and played with this apparatus and satisfied himself that he could move the overheads into a position that he required.

Thomas carefully selected the lowest of the forward gears and gently steered the vehicle around the yard in a practice run. He also operated the overhead gantry to a desired level of satisfaction. He slowly inched the apparatus out of the builders yard and drove slowly towards where he had planned to meet up with Henry.

Albert drove to the motel where McMillan was ensconced. He hoped that he wouldn't attract the attention of the local Guardia as he knew that he looked as if he was up to no good. He parked his car well away from the motel and made his way on foot and sat on a grassy verge looking at the hotel.

The motel had a huge billboard advertisement in the car park and Albert noted the telephone number of the hotel. Apart from a low light source emanating from the foyer of the motel the rest of the building was shrouded in darkness.

Albert rang the number of the hotel. After four rings the telephone was answered by the night receptionist. He sounded as if he had been sleeping and had just awoken.

Albert was relying on the fact that the receptionist could speak English.

'Hello, I am trying to make contact with my brother. He is English and he is staying at your hotel. His mobile is not working and I need to speak to him urgently. Our mother is not well and she is on a life-support machine in a hospital in London. I have to get back to the ward. Please write down this number and give it to him and tell him it is urgent. Do you understand?'

'Si senor, no problemo.'

Albert supplied a string of numbers chosen at random and terminated his call to the reception desk.

He sat and waited.

The room light went on in a ground floor room. It was one of the rooms that led directly into the motel car park.

Henry sat on a comfortable chaise-lounge awaiting a call from Thomas. The gang boss lay on the floor. His wide-open eyes kept darting from Henry to the door of the apartment fervently hoping that one of his bodyguards would come to his rescue.

Thomas was cursing the slowness of the vehicle. He had hoped to be in position before dawn broke. He had about 45 minutes to make the rendevouz with Henry.

Miguel Martine was awake at his usual early time of day. Miguel was a casual labourer who worked on the fruit farms just outside the town of Passina. He had to rise early in order to catch the workers' truck supplied by the farmer who owned the orange groves. He moved around his apartment silently in order not to wake his two young sons and his young wife.

As he was about to leave his flat, Miguel heard a low rumbling noise. He looked out of his small kitchen window and saw to his astonishment what was causing the rumbling noise.

Thomas had now eventually reached the edge of the town square of Passina. He took out his mobile and rang Henry.

'Your taxi is here, sir.'

Henry laughed but soon resumed his serious face and motioned to El Poderoso to get up off the floor. Henry grabbed him by the elbow and started to steer him out of the apartment. He suddenly stopped and said to the gang boss,

'Hang on a minute, you're not properly dressed.'

Henry took him back into his bedroom and picked up the blue cashmere scarf. He tied it tightly around his neck, almost choking him and continued to take him outside where he spotted Thomas clambering down out of the cabin to meet them.

Albert bided his time until the room light had been extinguished. He moved forward towards the car park door and carefully opened it. Once inside the building Albert waited for a few seconds until his eyes had adjusted to the low light. He moved down the corridor towards the room that he had worked out was occupied by McMillan.

There was no light visible below the door frame. Armed with his heavy duty torch in his left hand and his Glock pistol in his right hand Albert crashed through the flimsy door by using all his weight on his left shoulder. The door gave way easily.

Once inside the room, Albert shone his torch. The bed-clothes showed that the bed had been slept in but there was no occupant asleep or awake.

Albert hesitated. This hadn't been the plan. He had intended to take out McMillan and leave him to rot in this grubby room. Albert listened carefully but could not hear anything.

The room appeared to be empty. The net curtain by the French window moved slightly. Aiming at the curtain, Albert pulled it back to reveal that the window was open.

Albert climbed through the open window and headed in the direction of McMillan's car. The car was stationary. Albert checked that it was locked.

Albert strained his ears but the silence was deafening apart from a rustle of leaves from the trees in the car park. Suddenly, Albert heard a scraping sound. He looked towards the low wall that formed the perimeter of the car park.

Albert spotted a movement in the shadows. He raised his handgun. He presumed that McMillan was unarmed, else he would have been fired at by McMillan.

As Albert moved slowly towards the shadowy movement he was suddenly attacked by a figure which sprang at him from behind a large tree. Albert was knocked off balance but managed to retain hold of the firearm. Albert lifted the gun and pointed it at McMillan's forehead.

'Okay, do what you want, but do it quickly,' said McMillan.

'Not here,' replied Albert, 'back into your room.'

McMillan led the way with Albert following. The gun remained pointed at McMillan's back.

Henry Spearing was full of admiration for the driving skills of Thomas Cannon. Sat on the edge of the town square was the machinery that Thomas had driven under the cover of darkness from the building site to its present position.

The giant crane was now situated on the edge of the square with its long jib extending across the centre of the square.

El Poderoso saw the crane and started to shake uncontrollably. A length of rope in the form of a noose was placed and tightened around his neck by Henry. The rope was secured to the jib which had been lowered to ground level by Thomas.

Henry nodded to Thomas in the cab of the crane.

Very slowly the jib started to rise. The figure on the end of the rope was writhing frantically but after some twenty seconds all movement ceased.

Thomas continued to raise the jib until the suspended figure was swaying gently high above the town square.

Daylight was just beginning to break as Henry and Thomas quietly departed the scene. The early morning rays of the rising sun picked out the figure swaying on high.

As the town of Passina slowly awoke itself from the slumbers of the night the inhabitants were just about to realise that their lives were going to take a turn for the better. Small groups of people gathered on the edges of the square and were involved in animated discussion.

The early morning sun picked out the figure suspended from the jib. All doubt as to the identity of the corpse was removed at the sight of the blue cashmere scarf tied round the neck of the deceased.

Townsfolk pointed at the corpse and scarf. Some of the elderly men did their best to suppress a smile. Some successfully, others not. Young mothers taking children to school carefully averted the eyes of their youngsters but all conversation between the mothers was animated and excited.

McMillan led the way into his own room by way of the French windows. Albert closed the curtains and switched on the room light. The room consisted of a double bed, a wardrobe, a side table and a chair.

Albert sat McMillan down on the edge of the bed while he took up his position on the wooden chair. McMillan's eyes were wide open in fear.

In contrast, Albert didn't feel great. He was sweating profusely and he thought that was down to the items of clothing he was wearing, including the Kevlar bullet proof vest which weighed a few pounds.

McMillan noticed that Albert looked uncomfortable.

'You don't look very clever.'

'I'll still look better now than you will in a couple of minutes,' said Albert, but it was said in an unconvincing manner. Albert felt really ropey and lowered the gun away from McMillan's head.

McMillan noticed a change in Albert's constitution and he tried to seize the opportunity.

'This doesn't have to finish like this. You've been responsible for a series of brutal murders. You're no better than me but you can end it all here. Start all over again. Just walk away, get back to the UK. I'll crack on with my life here.'

'How do I know you won't have another pop at me,' said Albert. 'You thought you had killed me once and then killed my mate the priest, because you thought it was me.'

'It was only because of what happened to my mate Bill Cronk, but we can call it even. We both walk away and it all finishes here.'

Albert hesitated.

'You're probably right. I've had enough.'

McMillan's eyes lit up.

'What about the dog?' asked Albert.

'The one at the church, you mean?'

'Yes.'

McMillan remained silent and looked down at the floor. His shoulders slumped.

Albert guessed there and then that McMillan had poisoned the dog.

'You're right, though. Let's call it even,' said Albert.

McMillan's mood changed again for the better and he smiled.

'Only kidding,' said Albert, as he carefully raised the handgun and shot McMillan through his left eyeball.

The noise of the discharge had been suppressed. The entry point was small but the force of the bullet had created a large hole at the back of McMillan's head as a combination of blood, skin, tissue and bone hit the wall above the headboard of McMillan's bed.

Albert still felt groggy. Before leaving the room by the French windows he had a last look at McMillan. He was sprawled grotesquely on the bed, his one remaining eye staring at the ceiling.

'Nothing personal, but that's for Michael Creaney,' said Albert softly.

After switching off the room light he returned to his car and made his way back to the motorhome. He noticed that the huge Harley Davidson was sitting on its stand. He looked across to the restaurant part of the park where he spotted Henry and Thomas sitting nursing large mugs of coffee.

61.

The three men ordered breakfast and discussed what had to be done. Henry described the method and circumstances of the killing of El Poderoso.

'A proper slap then, Henry,' said Albert

'I've a little bit of tidying up to do,' said Henry, smiling. 'There were a few other casualties which I've managed to hide in the forest just outside the town. Perhaps we can scoop them up and get rid of them.'

'What do you want to do with them?' asked Albert.

'There's a pig farm just north of town. The animals will enjoy their breakfast just as much as us,' laughed Henry. 'Then I thought we would pay our respects to Brendan and pop down to the coast for a spot of lunch.'

Although Albert had seen and done a bit in the last few months he was taken aback with Henry's forthrightness.

'What about the bloke who's hanging about in the town square?' asked Thomas.

'We can leave him there as a tourist attraction and maybe as a warning to other wannabees,' replied Henry.

Albert said that he still didn't feel well and told his companions that he was going to have a lie down to try and shake off his nausea and lethargy.

Albert woke up after roughly three hours sleep but still felt below par. Henry and Thomas had returned to base camp.

'We've just fed the pigs,' said Henry, 'and now Thomas and I would like to take you out for a spot of lunch. We're all done here and we can treat it as an end of term celebration. What do you think, Albert?'

'I'm afraid I won't be much company in this state,' said Albert, 'but maybe the change of scenery will do me a bit of good.'

'Okay, we'll take one of the cars. I want to pay my final respects to Brendan and to show you where he is, then we can nip down to the coast and have something to eat. And maybe a few beers?' said Henry.

Albert volunteered to drive to take his mind off feeling poorly and was directed by Henry to Brendan's final resting place.

Albert was struck by the simple beauty of the grave marked by the small cairn of stones but was most impressed by the view from the top of the hill looking down to the shimmering blue sea in the distance.

Albert watched from the side as the two former soldiers stood with their arms round each other's shoulders. They bowed their heads in respect and after a minute or so joined Albert at the side of the cairn.

'All done,' said Henry, quietly.

Albert drove the three of them down to the Spanish seaside town. The car was parked in a side street and the three men strolled along the seafront. The resort was very busy, packed with tourists and excited children. The beach-wear shops were doing a roaring trade.

'I suppose you'll be wanting a bucket and spade?' said Henry to Thomas, laughing.

'Only to bury you in the sand,' he replied.

Henry led the way to a restaurant at the far end of the seafront. It looked a cut above the other restaurants. The three men chose a table out of the glaring sun. Henry and Thomas excitedly picked up the menus. Three large beers were ordered and when the waiter arrived for their order, Henry ordered enough tapas dishes to feed a regiment.

Albert sipped slowly at his beer but had no appetite for the grilled prawns and countless other dishes served up. Henry and Thomas made up for Albert's lack of appetite.

Albert excused himself and went inside to find the toilets. On his return to the table he caught sight of a tele-vision news channel behind the barmen's head in the bar area. He froze!

Staring back at him was a picture of himself. The photo-graph was one taken of him by the Spanish Guardia after the incident with William Cronk on a previous visit to Spain.

Albert shuffled back to the other two who by now, had finished the tapas and looked as if they were ready for another beer.

'We've got a major problem boys.'

Albert explained what he had just seen on the Spanish news programme.

'What did it say?' asked Thomas.

'My Spanish isn't that great,' replied Albert, 'but I don't

think it was complimentary.

Albert saw that Henry looked more worried than he had ever seen him before.

'Okay,' said Henry in a voice that suggested he was taking charge of the situation. 'I thought we might have had a few more days grace before the shit hit the fan but we'll need to instigate a cleaning up and clearing out process as soon as we can. Thomas can pay the bill to avoid any recognition and we'll get back to base. On the way back we can decide on a course of action.'

Thomas paid the bill at the bar with euros supplied by Albert who still controlled the finances.

Thomas also acted as driver on the way back to the Area de Rest.

On their return journey, Albert, who was sitting in the rear passenger seat, received a phone call from the UK.

'Good afternoon Albert. I've some bad news for you. The Spanish authorities have received information that you're responsible for a series of murders on the Spanish mainland, and in particular the area to the north of Valencia. They've recovered the body of Dennis McMillan and another body hanging above the town square of Passina. Their enquiries are now being concentrated at a pig farm just north of Passina. They've circulated your details and photograph to all police outlets and media channels. They are also interested in some maniac riding round Spain on a Harley Davidson, killing people at will. Please tell me those two things are not linked.'

'I'm afraid they are,' replied Albert. 'We're just heading back to camp after seeing my photograph on a news channel. I just need a bit of time to discuss things here and then I'll get back to you to tell you our plans.'

'You've got two hours.'

Albert relayed the conversation to the other two.

'I'm not going back to the UK,' said Thomas. 'I'm going to take my chances out here. I like the weather, the food and the beer.'

'We'll form a partnership,' said Henry, 'we're capable of hiding in the country and lying low for a while. We can survive on the land as far as food is concerned and when everything dies down we can get stuck into the black labour market. Don't worry about us, Albert.'

Albert thought about it for a moment. The two of them might get away with it but three of them made it more dangerous and there would be a strong likelihood of being caught.

'I might try to get back to the UK,' said Albert, 'But I'll wait to see what my contact in the UK says. There's also the small matter of finances. As you know, this operation was subsidised with the intention of getting rid of McMillan. Now that's been achieved I feel that the rest of the money is ours.'

'Agreed.' said Henry.

'I'll need some to get me out of Spain. I'll give the pair of you a large whack of Euros to get you started on your new life.'

'Sounds like a plan,' said Thomas, smiling.

'One bit of bad news though Henry. The motorbike has been compromised and you won't be able to use it. We have a bit of clearing up to do when we get back. Any suggestions?'

'Thomas can follow me in one of the hired cars to my secure garage. We can dump the munitions and bike in the garage. I have a spare set of forged plates I can put on the hire car. That takes care of us. The motorhome can be torched after we have taken out what we need.'

Back at the rest area. Albert went through the motorhome and packed a small canvas bag of clothing. Henry stored all necessary munitions and clothing in the boot of the hire car they intended to use.

Albert's phone rang.

'You need to get yourself out of that area as soon as possible. You need to get yourself to Bilbao before next Monday and when you get there ring me on this number. The financier's concerned about being compromised. That cannot happen. Do you understand that? If you want to live, don't fuck this up. What are the other two boneheads going to do?'

'They plan on disappearing into the sunset and living off the land for a while until the dust settles. They're more than capable of looking after themselves.'

Where are they going?'

Albert hesitated thinking that this was a strange question. What difference did it make where they were going to disappear to?

'Portugal I think, but if they put their mind to it nobody will find them.'

The caller appeared satisfied.

'I should add that if anybody is thinking about any funny business I've instituted a plan whereby if anything happens to any one of us, the authorities in Spain and the

UK will get to know the truth of the matter.'

Albert hoped that this bluff would work as Ted Fuller knew that Albert was capable of such a threat judged on experiences in the past.

The caller paused on the other end of the line. Albert presumed he'd given him food for thought.

'Okay, get yourself to Bilbao and ring me. Don't fuck this up.'

Albert relayed the gist of the conversation to the other two.

'We're going to have to change your appearance, Albert. You stand out like a sore thumb.'

Albert was plonked into one of the plastic chairs next to the outdoor table under the awning of the motorhome.

A towel was placed round his neck by Thomas whilst Henry soaped the top of his head into a thick lather. Thomas appeared with his cut throat razor and proceeded to scalp Albert who sat bemused in the chair.

He thought to himself that nothing seemed to faze these two and that the whole adventure had been part of a big game. He knew though, that he could trust these two with his life.

Once Thomas had finished with the razor, Henry cleaned and polished the top of Albert's dome. With a matador's swirl he waved the towel above his head and said,

'That'll be fifteen pounds sir, and would sir like anything for the weekend?'

The three of them giggled like young schoolboys. Thomas held up a shaving mirror. Albert couldn't believe what he was looking at. The new image aged him by about fifteen years but he was happy that he now didn't look like the mugshot doing the rounds on Spanish television broadcasts.

'It won't take long to grow back,' said Thomas, smiling.

62.

The first shot sounded like a twig snapping. A large chunk of Henry's scalp became detached from his cranium and his huge torso crumpled in an ungainly heap, throwing up a shower of dust.

Henry Spearing lay dead in the hot Spanish sun. Blood had seeped from the head wound and surrounded what was left of his skull. His black sleek hair with silvery strands was matted with blood and mucus. The Lion of Iraq and Northern Ireland lay dead on Spanish soil.

El Nariz, from Caballo's gang had always prided himself as an expert sniper. He had always wanted to follow in the footsteps of his grandfather who had acted as such in the Spanish Civil war. He peered through the trees into the car park to choose his next target.

When Thomas and Albert had watched Henry fall to the floor they looked at each other and held each other's eyes.

Thomas knew from previous experience in the desert that having a sniper on your side was a prized asset. He knew that the sniper would have to choose between himself and Albert. He screamed at Albert to run while he ran in an opposite direction in an attempt to distract and confuse the shooter.

Albert ran furiously towards the motorhome and used it as cover but knew that this could only be temporary. Behind the motorhome was a drainage ditch which Albert rolled into. The concrete ditch was dry but provided some cover.

Trying to put distance between himself and the sniper he crawled as fast as his legs and arms would allow in the circumstances. He heard another sharp crack and a yell of pain.

By using the drainage ditch Albert made it to the restaurant and once at the rear of the restaurant he began to climb the wooded hill.

Halfway up the steep slope Albert looked down to the car park. He saw the sprawled figure of Thomas lying in the dust with blood seeping from a large neck wound.

His good friend, Thomas Cannon, had also perished. Not in the deserts of the Middle East or the rolling hills of Antrim, but in a scruffy car park rest area used by tourists and lorry drivers.

Albert tried to distance himself as far as possible from the shooter. From the top of the hill he looked down again to the car park. A gang of locusts were scavenging the car park.

He watched as the two dead bodies were frisked. The motorhome was looted before being set on fire. Before Albert looked away he saw one of the gang riding away on the Harley Davidson.

63.

Albert scrambled down the other side of the hill. In the distance he saw a minor road with the occasional vehicle travelling slowly.

Albert sat and had a quick inventory of his possessions. The only clothes he had were the ones he was wearing. At least he had the remainder of the Euros supplied by the Irishman, Doyle. He had a few Euro notes loose in his pocket and the rest of the Euros were wrapped in a polythene package and taped to his stomach underneath his shirt. He still had the mobile phone. He didn't have his passport which was probably a good thing.

Albert knew the situation was serious. Firstly he had to get away from this area and think about getting to Bilbao.

Albert scrambled down the hill. He had to be careful on his choice of transport as there was a good chance that the killers were still in the area.

Albert hid himself behind a large clump of bushes and was able to see approaching vehicles. He allowed a dirty dusty saloon car to pass, followed by a worker's van. Behind the van he spotted a tractor pulling a cart full of cabbages.

He stepped out from behind the bushes and in sign language which was recognised internationally, indicated with his thumb in the direction of travel.

The driver of the tractor was an elderly overweight farmer. He was wearing a battered old Panama hat and slumped over the wheel. He indicated to Albert to jump into the cart. Gratefully Albert climbed in beside his new travelling companions, a cartful of produce heading for the local market at the next town.

Albert was careful to conceal himself. The lack of suspension in the cart reminded Albert of previous journeys made in the prison van journeys between HMP Belmarsh and the Central Criminal Court. Albert didn't think there was a lot to choose between the comfort of the two vehicles but marginally preferred the one he was now travelling in.

When Albert poked his head up over the side of the cart he saw that they were approaching what looked like a fairly large town. The tractor slowed down at the entrance to a market square. The farmer came round to uncouple the cart. Albert climbed out and jumped to the ground. He thanked the farmer and then he pointed to the farmer's Panama hat. Albert rubbed his now bald head and proffered a ten-Euro note to the farmer. The farmer couldn't believe his luck and immediately removed his headwear and handed it to Albert in exchange for the hat. Little did he realise that Albert's offer was for the lift away from danger. The farmer thought he had given a lift to someone who had just escaped from a mental institution.

Albert walked to a mall of shops and entered a gent's outfitters. When he emerged back out into the bright sunlight

Albert was transformed. A complete change of shirt and linen trousers together with a change of underwear.

His old clothes and the Panama hat were dumped in a rubbish bin at the rear of the store. Albert was now sporting a plain white baseball cap and had also picked up a couple of COVID face masks. Albert had never been worried about wearing them in the peak of the pandemic but now sensibly thought the wearing of one would help in avoiding recognition.

Albert's next port of call was to the bus station which he had seen signposted. Wearing his mask and cap he approached the ticket desk situated at the back of the entrance hall. He asked for a single ticket to Madrid, figuring that he would have no trouble getting to Bilbao by rail from the Spanish capital.

The journey itself was pleasant enough. The coach was air-conditioned and the scenery, especially in the mountain sections, was spectacular.

But Albert was disturbed. He now had time to contemplate what had happened over the last few hours. He got quite upset thinking about Henry and Thomas. Two men who had turned out to be good friends, especially Thomas. And, of course, he couldn't forget Brendan. The death of his good friend Father Michael Creaney had also happened because of his connection to him. Albert realised with dawning horror that he was the centrepin of all these deaths. There were also the deaths of the low-lifes on the periphery but he didn't allow himself to get too upset at their passing. They had it coming to them.

Albert wondered what the future held for him. He didn't

know what plans were in store for him at Bilbao. Where was he going to finish up? Would Doyle be threatened by his existence and arrange for him to be taken out? Doyle didn't know of course that Albert did not have a protection plan processed. Albert thought he could trust Detective Sergeant Ted Fuller but wasn't a hundred percent convinced.

As the coach pulled into the main bus station in Madrid, Albert decided he would spend the evening in the capital city before catching a train to Bilbao the next morning.

He still had an excess of Euros and therefore took the decision that he wasn't going to skimp on home comforts. He chose an expensive looking luxury hotel but before booking a room he bought another change of clothes and a canvas carry bag.

The room was air-conditioned and after soaking in a huge bath for an hour Albert ordered room service. He spent a relaxing restful night in the Spanish capital.

Albert's proposed early night was interrupted by the ringing of his mobile phone.

'I'm sorry about your friends. But, with the best will in the world the way they operated meant that they were never going to make old bones.'

'I suppose that's one way of putting it,' replied Albert.

'I presume you have Euros left, Albert?'

'Yes I have.'

'Right, when you get to Bilbao tomorrow you need to get yourself to the port area. It's a bit rough down there. You need to find a bar called La Luna. It's for lowlifes so you should have no trouble fitting in,' said the voice with a chuckle.

'Very funny. What happens then?'

'You have to find a man called Karla spelt with a 'K', introduce yourself as Albert and leave the rest to him. Any questions?'

'Who killed my two mates?'

'They were taken out by a gang run by a menace called El Caballo. Unfortunately for the gang they were under surveillance by a crack Spanish Police surveillance team who had been looking at them. The sniper who assassinated your two mates was wasted by the surveillance team when he wouldn't put down the rifle. Well, that's the official story, if you get my drift? The rest of the gang were scooped up and face a few years in a Spanish jail.'

'Are you saying that the surveillance team just sat back and watched as they tried to kill us?'

'Yep. They had guessed who you three were and thought they could kill two birds with one stone. They did kill two birds but one of them flew the nest. You!'

'Your sense of humour doesn't become you. Is that all?'

'That's it as far as I'm concerned. A good result for my man. McMillan is dead. A couple of Spanish gangs get taken out so he will be able to call in some favours from certain Spanish influencers in the future. A threat to him being compromised has disappeared with the SAS unit being taken care of. Which leaves you. He either likes you or doesn't know what you've got on him. So he's anxious to get you somewhere where he can keep an eye on you and weigh you up.'

'It won't surprise you to know that I've got something on

him that'll finish him. I'm sure you'll keep that to yourself.'

'Goodnight Albert.'

'Goodnight Sergeant.'

64.

Early next morning Albert took a cab to the northern outskirts of Madrid and was dropped off at the Estacion de Chamartin. Wearing a covid face mask with his new baseball cap pulled down onto his head he purchased a single train ticket to Bilbao. He scooped up a fresh hot coffee and a slab of tortilla and took up his window seat for the journey which was advertised as taking over four hours.

The seat next to him remained empty and the two seats opposite him were taken up by an elderly woman and a younger version who Albert presumed to be her daughter. Albert felt safe enough to remove his covid mask and spent the early part of the journey admiring the Spanish scenery.

He was worried about his personal situation. Could he trust Detective Sergeant Fuller and was he at the bidding of Aiden Doyle? Doyle was obviously a powerful figure and had the means and the where-with-all to get rid of Albert at any given time. Albert could easily have remained in Spain and taken his chances, but with Thomas and Henry being murdered he felt he had no choice but to follow the instructions which had been meted out by Ted Fuller.

Albert took advantage of the trolley wagon to eat on the

train journey as he couldn't be sure of what adventures lay ahead of him.

The train pulled into Bilbao Abando station. As Albert alighted from the train he noticed a welcome difference in temperature from that of the stifling heat of the Spanish capital.

Albert had time to kill before looking up Karla. He decided that a visit to the city's Guggenheim museum would fill in the afternoon.

When he left the air-conditioned building he hailed a cab and asked to be dropped off at the port area. The sun was beginning to disappear and the Port area took on a more menacing feel. The fumes of diesel and fish pervaded the air.

Albert walked for a few blocks until he noticed the bar called La Luna. Fuller was right when he said it looked seedy. Albert didn't think it looked that good!

The bright neon lighting flashed out the name of the bar. Albert went to the door at the side of the premises. He knocked on the heavy steel door. It was opened by a bruiser who was holding out his hand for the entry fee. Albert paid him 10 euros.

Once inside the building Albert took his time to allow his eyes to adjust to the low lighting. He saw a bar at the far end of the sweaty, humid room with two of the high backed bar stools occupied by two men nursing beers.

Albert looked to the right and saw a small stage occupied by two women who were dancing to a suggestive soundtrack. Albert was not impressed by either their looks or the quality of their dance routine, a fact backed up by the group of men on the other side of the bar watching a Spanish football match on a giant wall-mounted television screen.

Albert placed his canvas bag on the floor and took up occupancy of one of the available high backed bar stools. He was approached by the bartender. He was in his fifties with a large paunch. His dyed black greasy hair was swept over his scalp. He was unshaven. He granted Albert a disingenuous smile. Apart from the teeth that were coloured yellow and black, he possessed a fine set of dentures. His smile revealed the odd gap in the upper gum.

'Senor, how can I be of assistance to you?'

'I'm looking for someone called Karla.'

'This is your lucky day Senor, for you now have the privilege of speaking to that very person. You must be the Englishman.'

'I am. I have been told that you can help me.'

'Indeed I can Mister Albert. We now have to discuss how you wish to travel. You can travel either de-luxe or economy. The choice will be yours, Senor.'

'What is the difference?' asked Albert

'The difference is 4000 Euros. For 8000 Euros you have room service and an en-suite toilet. For 4000 Euros the conditions are not so good. The accommodation is very basic.'

Albert had enough of Doyle's finances to afford the deluxe but didn't want to put himself at risk by extracting the cash from his money belt in front of the clientele. He excused himself and went to the washrooms. The highly pungent smells were awful but Albert entered a cubicle and peeled off the necessary travelling expenses.

Somebody entered the rest room and Albert had a fleeting moment of panic. Was this where it was all going to end? Stabbed or shot in a cubicle in a smelly toilet in a grubby nightclub in a northern Spanish port?

The visitor to the toilets did what he had to do and left. Albert breathed a sigh of relief. He returned to the bar area and called Karla over.

'What happens now?' asked Albert.

'First of all you pay for your luxury trip.'

Albert handed Karla 8,000 euros.

'In two hours, you and I will go for a little walk. I will take you to your transport. In the meantime you can have a beer or something to eat. You can watch the delightful ladies going through their routines.'

Albert decided to watch what was left of the televised football match.

Two hours later Karla signalled to Albert to follow him out of the bar. The two burlesque dancers were now performing their second stint.

As Albert passed by them one of the artistes flashed Albert a smile. A smile that contained less teeth than Karla. Albert wondered if Bilbao had a dentistry problem. At least the toothless wonder had more going for her than her overweight companion who sported the trace of a moustache and a five-o-clock shadow.

Albert was pleased to escape the smells and dowdiness of the night club. It would remain high on his list of places never to visit again.

Karla led the way with Albert following a step behind.

The dock area was shrouded in darkness save for flood-lights which picked out cranes loading containers onto large cargo boats.

As the two men approached the dock area Albert saw that the docking area was fenced off. Karla took Albert to the left hand side of the fencing where a dark uniformed security guard slouched against the fencing, He was holding on to the leash which had attached to it a ferocious looking German Shepherd dog.

Karla nodded at the guard who returned his greeting in a similar fashion. Karla handed the guard an envelope and then opened a wired gate. Karla prodded Albert through the gateway.

'Adios, Senor.'

Karla disappeared in the direction he had just come from.

Albert waited just inside the gate. The guard indicated to him to stand in the shadows of a huge green metal shipping container. Five minutes later a figure appeared from the direction of the giant ship.

The man was in his mid forties and sported a black bushy beard which had been shaped to the contours of his lower face. He was dressed in black. A short black denim jacket, black trousers and shoes and a dark blue shirt which displayed the motif of the shipping company he worked for. Albert thought he recognised the national flag of Cuba from the motif.

Blackbeard spoke to the guard. An envelope was handed over and Blackbeard indicated to Albert to follow him. Albert followed the man up a steep gangway and at the top of the gangway a breathless Albert saw that he was on board a ship. He was taken through a heavy metal doorway on the deck.

'I am the captain of this ship. My name is Captain Alves,' said the man in perfect English. 'Whilst you are on my boat you will obey the rules. There is only one rule. You will do as you are told at all times.'

'Where are we going?'

'It is something you should not be concerned about. The most important thing is that you will no longer be in Spain where your life, apparently, is at risk. Follow me.'

Albert wasn't so sure about his life not being at risk but dutifully followed Captain Alves down a series of metal stairs. After descending numerous flights Albert found that they were in a space entirely made up of engine parts, metal piping and gauges. The pipes hissed and spat out steam. The space was claustrophobic and the noise was deafening.

'Welcome to your living quarters, Mister Oxford.'

'I thought I had paid for de-luxe accommodation, Captain,' said Albert.

'You have sir. This is the best room in the hotel. Your bed's over there,' pointing to a straw mattress on the oily floor. 'Your toilet requisites are accommodated by that means.'

Albert noticed a shiny metal pail at the other end of the network of metal pipes.

'That will be emptied twice a day when your food is brought to you. We will supply you with a towel free of charge and I see that you have with you a change of clothing. Can I suggest you keep that clean until you need it.'

'How long will we be at sea?' asked Albert.

'Hopefully only two days but a storm has been forecast for the Bay of Biscay so it will depend on the severity of the storm.'

Albert's gloom was not lightened by this news but at least he knew now that the ship was heading in a northerly direction.

65.

Albert wondered what he had let himself in for. There was nothing he could do but to get on with it. He fluffed up his mattress and lay back with his arms behind his head.

In this particular prison cell he had no idea of time or date. The noises of the hissing engines would prevent meaningful sleep. Albert gave great thought to what he had been through the last few months of his life.

From a humdrum existence living in east London he had progressed past the deaths of numerous people who had been unfortunate to cross his path. Here he was now as a stowaway on a ship attempting to escape the Spanish judicial system after he and his friends had caused mayhem in Spain.

McMillan was dead, as was the crime boss and a few of his henchmen, but so were three friends. He would especially miss Thomas who he had grown close to. Albert had thought that Henry and Brendan were on a death wish and that this adventure was possibly a last hurrah for them both. But not so Thomas.

Albert also thought about Father Michael Creaney, a

man that Albert could easily have been friends with for the rest of his life. He thought fleetingly about Helen and her natural beauty and her rare shy smiles. He wondered what she would be doing now and where she was.

Helen was Albert's last image as he drifted off into sleep but was soon awoken with a shuddering noise and a noticeable increase in the hissing and spitting of the engines in his de-luxe accommodation. The boat had obviously cast off and was manoeuvering.

The movement of the boat made Albert nauseous. He made early use of the metal pail. Albert felt that this would be a long two days.

Sure enough the ship listed and rolled sideways as well as up and down. Machines clanked. Albert was thankful for the metal bucket. Sleep was impossible and the next few hours seemed to go on forever.

Over the non-stop noise of the engines Albert was suddenly aware of another man in his private bedroom. He was dressed in a navy blue boiler suit and was wearing a mask over his face. In one of his hands he was carrying a mug of what smelled like coffee and in his other hand he had a bread roll wrapped in grease-proof paper.

Albert could not face the prospect of eating anything and indicated to the sailor that he didn't want the food. The sailor smiled and put the package into one of the deep pockets of his boiler suit. Albert was grateful for the coffee and placed it on the floor next to his bed of straw.

Albert's butler then picked up the bucket and exited through a metal door on the other side of Albert's living quarters. He returned a couple of minutes later and re-locked the door. The bucket was wet and smelled of sea water. The masked man smiled at Albert with his eyes and retired from the bedroom.

The captivity did not get any easier for Albert although it appeared that the forecast storm did not materialise. Offers of food were turned down to the obvious delight of his man-servant who availed himself of the extra rations. Albert existed on a diet of coffee for two days. He was also grateful for the regular emptying of the metal bucket.

After what had seemed an interminable journey, the engine noise began to recede and the movement of the ship had seemed to slow. Albert suspected that the ship was nearing the end of its journey. This was confirmed when Captain Alves entered Albert's living space.

'We will be docking soon, Mister Oxford. But you will not be allowed to leave the ship until your escort has arrived. In the meantime I suggest you shower and change into your fresh clothes.'

Albert was escorted to the crew's quarters where he spent an age scrubbing himself clean. He felt a different person now that he had dressed and once he was away from the engine room, he took advantage of the cheese bread roll that was offered.

06.

As Albert emerged onto the deck he could see that darkness had descended. Floodlights picked out cranes removing huge green containers from the upper deck area and swinging them round and placing them on the back section of articulated lorries.

A slight drizzle of rain descended from the dark sky. Albert quite welcomed the softness of the moisture after the heat of the Iberian peninsula.

Captain Alves escorted Albert down the gangplank. As Albert stepped onto the quay Captain Alves said to him,

'If you walk to the end of that chain link fence, you will see a security guard who will allow you through. Once you are through that gate you will be met by another escort. Good luck. I hope you enjoyed your trip.'

'I can't say I would use the word *enjoy* but I'll leave a favourable rating on TripAdvisor. I'll also report favourably on the quality of the room service and in particular my personal butler.'

Captain Alves looked bemused but grabbed Albert's hand and shook it firmly.

'Can I just ask one question?' said Albert.

'You may,' replied the captain.

'If I was travelling in deluxe class, what sort of accommodation would you provide as economy class?'

Alves pointed to one of the green containers being lowered by crane onto the back platform of an articulated lorry.

Albert shuddered.

As Albert walked through the drizzle to the end of the fencing he took stock of his surroundings. One of the flags flying above the dock he recognised as the tricolour of the Republic of Ireland. Albert noticed a sign indicating that he was now walking towards territory which was marked as Dublin Port Authority.

When Albert reached the end of the fencing, a gate was opened by a guard. No words were exchanged but the guard pointed in the direction of a large black saloon car sitting at the far end of the quay. The vehicle had its side-lights on and occasionally the windscreen wipers would clear the drizzle from the screen. Albert walked slowly towards the vehicle. He felt apprehensive.

When he reached the large car the rear door opened. No one emerged so Albert took that as an invitation to enter the car.

Sat behind the steering wheel was a sharp-suited type who Albert recognised as one of the employees of Aidan Doyle.

'The boss wants to see you.'

Nothing else was said. Albert relaxed into the comfort of the leather seats. Questioning the driver would be fruitless so he would save his questions for Doyle.

After a twenty minute journey the car pulled onto the driveway of a very impressive hotel on the outskirts of Dublin. Albert was led through to a deserted lounge area dominated by large leather high backed chairs. Two elegant sofas were placed either side of an expensive low glass-topped coffee table.

As Albert passed one of the chairs he was suddenly aware of a figure sitting in the chair, A diminutive shape. That of Aidan Doyle.

'Good evening Mister Oxford,' said Doyle in a soft Irish accent. 'Welcome to Ireland. I trust your journey was pleasant and that you were able to take in the views and partake of the fine restaurant on board?'

Albert didn't answer.

'First things first. Thank you for carrying out the task that we had agreed on.'

'My pleasure,' said Albert.

'But now we move on to matters more disturbing. Your activities have ruffled a few Spanish feathers and the authorities in Spain have a price on your head. That means, effectively, that you're a prisoner here in the Republic as any attempted entry to the British mainland would see you chained and handcuffed and returned to spend the rest of your life rotting in a Spanish jail. My spotless reputation could be in jeopardy. But of course, if you keep your nose clean, you can enjoy a certain amount of freedom here in this beautiful country.'

'What happens now then?' asked Albert.

'A very good friend of mine called Malachi, owns a large farm in the countryside. Malachi was also a close friend of

Michael Creaney. In fact the three of us grew up together. We went our separate ways but we always remained the closest of friends. Malachi will employ you and provide you with lodging.'

Albert considered this and thought this was as good an offer as he was going to get. It meant that his fear of Doyle disposing of him had dissipated. The offer would suffice in the short term until Albert decided what way the future would develop.

'There's another reason of course, why I want Malachi to look after you. You're a threat to my reputation and my good name. I have a hold on you, but as yet I don't know what steps you've taken to protect your own existence. Once I'm satisfied that you pose no threat to me we'll discuss your future. However, should you pose such a threat to me, my business, or my reputation I'll deal with it. Do I make myself clear?'

Albert nodded.

'What happens now.'

'You'll spend tonight in this magnificent hotel. After breakfast you'll be taken by my man, here, to a shopping area in Dublin where you'll be fitted out with the basics that you require. You'll then be taken to meet Malachi on his farm in the countryside. I'll personally escort you. I need to catch up with my old friend.'

67.

The following morning after a large breakfast Albert was taken by the minder to the shopping outlet. The minder paid for all the items with what was obviously the company credit card.

When Albert returned to the hotel he sat at one of the outside tables in the shade of a jacaranda tree. He was joined on the terrace by Doyle who ordered coffee for them.

Doyle invited Albert to tell him in detail about the killing of McMillan. Doyle listened intently and hung on every word uttered by Albert. At the end of the account Doyle permitted himself a smile of quiet satisfaction.

Doyle then instructed Albert to pick up his belongings from his room and then asked him to accompany him to his limousine. Both men sat in the rear seats of the big comfortable saloon while the driver undertook the four hour drive into the middle of Ireland.

During the journey Albert was asked by Doyle to tell him about Albert's travelling companions in Spain.

Albert provided every detail and was profusive in his praise of the three men that he had recruited. Doyle appeared satisfied. The rest of the journey was made in comparative silence.

During the drive Albert was captivated by the beauty of the countryside. Everything was so green. Not just green, but countless shades of green, light and dark, soft and bright.

They passed through countless villages, the focal point of each seeming to be premises primarily existing for the sale and purchase of alcohol.

One of the villages that they passed through struck a chord with Albert. He thought it had been mentioned by his late friend Father Creaney but couldn't be sure.

Eventually the big car swung into a smaller road barely wide enough to accommodate the saloon. The car stopped at a gate which the driver had to open. Once the car was through, the gate was re-closed and the car and occupants continued their journey to a large sprawling single-storey farmhouse. On the way to the house Albert saw that most of the fields were planted with crops or grain. In a field far off to the left, grazed a herd of cattle.

The farmhouse consisted of a whitewashed building. Another whitewash was overdue. A large imposing oak door in the centre of the facade opened and out stepped a man, presumably Malachi.

Doyle and the man greeted each other with a warm embrace.

'Malachi, this is the man we talked about, Albert Oxford. I would like him to be in your care for the immediate future.'

Malachi extended his forearm to Albert. He shook hands

with Albert with a strong firm grip. Malachi was not tall but was well proportioned and his muscular frame had obviously been honed by hard work on the farm. His chiselled face was weather beaten and he possessed a firm square jaw. His hair was greying and cut very short to his scalp. He wore the clothes of a farmer.

Doyle and his henchman were invited in for tea but Doyle declined, stating that he had to get back to Dublin and then eventually to London.

Albert retrieved his shopping from the boot of the car and shook hands with Doyle before he got into his car.

68.

O ver the next few days Albert discovered that Malachi was not much of a conversationalist. Albert learned that he had once been married but his wife had become disillusioned with the prospect of spending the rest of her life on a farm in a remote part of Ireland. She had left Malachi some 12 years previously.

The farmhouse consisted of three separate living quarters. Albert took up occupancy of one. It was sparsely furnished with a wash basin, bed and wardrobe. Thin curtains hung at the solitary window. Albert's toilet was an outside toilet which wouldn't be much fun during the cold winter months ahead. An outside cubicle provided facilities to shower but at least the water temperature reached a height that made showering almost bearable. The farm's kitchen was basic with a cooker and fridge. An oak table with four oak chairs was the centrepiece.

Albert had been shown round the rest of the farm. He was attended by two collie sheepdogs. The outhouses contained a variety of farming equipment including two ageing tractors. Other storage sheds contained grass and hay for feeding livestock. Apart from the herd of cows

Albert had noticed a field of sheep grazing contendly. A chicken run contained a dozen hens who consistently provided the raw materials for breakfast. Another barn contained fairly modern equipment for milking the cows.

Albert was staggered by the size of the farm and the amount of work it would take to keep it running but was reassured by Malachi that a couple of youths from the village were relied on for casual labour.

69.

O ver the course of the next few weeks Albert had settled into a happy routine. Malachi had taught him the rudiments of operating a tractor and instructed Albert on the finer points of working the land with the tractor attachments.

Albert was also shown how to attach the udders of the cow to the milking machines and was surprised how much milk could be taken from one animal. With the assistance of the two sheep dogs the sheep were moved from one field to another. Malachi was a good teacher and there was nothing about farming that he didn't know.

'This is a huge never-ending job Malachi. Do you never get fed up with it?' asked Albert.

'What else would I do?' the farmer replied. Show me another job better than this. You work in the open air growing your own food. The farm is set in the most beautiful countryside and I don't have to answer to anybody.'

'That's very true Malachi.' Albert thought for a few seconds, 'Isn't it about time I called you by your first name?'

My name is Malachi, and that's it.'

The routine over the next few weeks didn't vary much. Albert's highlight of the week was a Saturday evening when he would accompany his landlord to the local hostelry to partake in the quaffing of several pints of Guinness. Albert, by now, had been converted to the black stuff.

He was also captivated by the musicians with their fiddles accompanying anybody who wanted to stand up and sing.

On one occasion Albert asked Malachi about his friendship with Michael Creaney and Aidan Doyle.

'We were three kids who grew up together. We were inseparable, but as you get older you diverge. We still remained strong friends. Aidan saw an opportunity to make a better life for himself in finance and although he's a bigshot now he's remained a very true and loyal friend. Michael found the big G'

'Guinness, you mean,' asked Albert.

Malachi laughed out loud. The first time Albert had witnessed that.

'No, not that one. The other big G up in the sky.'

With Sunday being strictly observed by Malachi as a day of rest, Albert took to improving his home comforts. On one of the trips to the market town Albert purchased a radio. Despite the poor signal in the area, Albert constructed a home-made aerial and was therefore able to listen to his favourite classical music station.

The working week saw Albert aboard one of the tractors cultivating the land. His education in farming was continued with Malachi being a keen instructor and Albert being a receptive student.

Although Malachi was a very quiet man he had taken a shine to Albert. He enjoyed his humour and sat enthralled as Albert described what life had been like in east London.

'I can see why you are enjoying life on the farm Albert. What a terrible existence.'

'It seemed okay at the time, Malachi, but this place and lifestyle is bliss. Thank you for allowing me to stay here and prosper.'

Malachi didn't reply immediately but seemed to be considering what he wanted to say.

'Albert, I've had to report back to Aidan Doyle. He had asked me to monitor you and assess your potential threat to his reputation but I've told him that in my opinion you pose no such threat and that you would be welcome to move on should you wish.'

'That was very decent of you to say that Malachi. I have to say though, that I'm in no rush to move anywhere. In any event, who would help you with the lambing in the Spring?'

'How do you think I managed before you came along?' smiled Malachi.

'I don't see how you could have managed without the assistance of the second best farmer in Ireland,' retorted Albert.

There followed another rare laugh from the Irishman.

'I've an outing planned for next Wednesday, Albert. Father Creaney's body is buried not far from here. Only a few miles away. The man didn't have a proper funeral because of Covid restrictions so a few of his friends are going to meet up and celebrate his life. You're very welcome to come with me.'

'I'd love to,' said Albert.

Albert had a recurring nagging thought. How would he be received by the locals when they became aware of his involvement in the death of Michael Creaney?

Albert confided with Malachi but was reassured by the Irish farmer.

'You underestimate the intelligence of this community, Albert. Maybe someone has let it slip that you were somehow involved with the death of Father Michael's killer'. Malachi gave Albert one of his rare smiles.

The following Wednesday Albert donned his only suit. Malachi looked the smartest Albert had ever seen him.

Malachi took the wheel of the fifteen year old Ford and drove them to the village where Malachi, Aidan Doyle and Michael Creaney had grown up.

The sun shone brightly on the cemetery on the outskirts of the village. The shadow of the church steeple fell across the gravestones save for one which was picked out by the rays of the sun.

Over two hundred people had converged on this hamlet to celebrate the life of someone they had held close to their hearts and whom they regarded as one of their own.

Albert stood at the back of the crowd. There was no religious element to the event but Aidan Doyle delivered a heartfelt and moving speech about his late friend. Moments of humour were introduced by Doyle including the fact that Michael Creaney had found cricket late in his life. Albert smiled.

Albert looked round the assembled gathering. The

audience was hanging on every word Doyle was saying, straining to hear the amusing anecdotes. At the end of his speech Doyle said very simply,

'God bless you and look after you, Michael Creaney.'

The assembled gathering burst into spontaneous applause. Albert looked to his right. He couldn't believe what he had seen.

Standing at the back of the gathering below a large oak tree was a woman dabbing her eye with a handkerchief. Dressed in a simple dark blue dress and without a discernible trace of make-up was someone Albert never expected to see again.

Albert's heart pounded. She was as beautiful as ever. She was standing on her own and, as the crowd began to make its way to the village hall, Albert lost sight of her.

Albert was swept up in the crowd on the way to the hall. Albert was hoping desperately that Helen would be at the celebration and on entering the hall he craned anxiously to spot her. He went back outside but only managed to catch a glimpse of her in the backseat of a vehicle belonging to a local taxi firm. The car drove out of the village.

Disappointed beyond belief, Albert returned to the hall. The main floor had been cleared of tables and chairs. The chairs had been placed round three of the walls whilst the fourth wall was lined by a series of trestle tables piled high with partly poured pints of Guinness. Another table was adorned by all manner of food and on the stage a group was setting up its musical instruments ready to entertain the throng.

Before long the party was in full swing but Albert was

not enjoying the celebration. He couldn't stop thinking about the woman he had just seen.

Albert's thoughts were interrupted by Aidan Doyle.

'I've been told that you are enjoying yourself, Mister Oxford and that you have taken to the joys of farming. Malachi enjoys your company and he said he will be sorry to see you go. I would urge you to consider the danger of attempting to return to England as my man tells me that you are still a person of considerable interest as far as the authorities are concerned. If I had the choice of working the land with Malachi or languishing in a Spanish jail then I'm afraid there would be no choice in the matter.'

'Mister Doyle, there's no chance of me returning to England. I'm very happy here in my newly adopted country.'

'I must say you don't look that happy. You look as if you've just seen a ghost.'

'You could say that. I've just seen a person from my previous life. Someone who was looked after by Michael Creaney.

'Ah, you mean the girl who wanted to be a nun. Helen, I think her name is.'

'You know her?' asked Albert.

'I do indeed. She lives only a few miles from here on a small holding that belonged to her parents.'

The party looked destined to continue into the small hours of the next day but Malachi and Albert had farm animals to tend to and other farm work needed progressing.

The journey back in the car was made in silence.

70.

SIX MONTHS LATER

Albert sat on the wooden park bench gazing down at the grave stones scattered below him. Although not a religious man he had promised himself that he would regularly visit the grave of his friend. He owed him an immeasurable debt. Dark grey clouds scudded across the horizon bringing with them the threat of heavy rain.

The woman sitting next to him placed her hand on top of his.

'Time to go I think, Albert.'

Hand in hand the two of them walked up the grassy path to the metal gate at the top of the cemetery. Albert got behind the wheel of the truck and drove the pair of them back home just as the first of the raindrops landed on the windscreen.

Mister Albert Oxford and Mrs Helen Oxford had only been married for four weeks. She had worn a simple white dress with a hairband made from wild flowers. He was dressed in a brand new dark suit. His black shoes were highly polished and he wore an open necked white shirt.

The wedding and subsequent celebration was paid for by Aidan Doyle. Malachi was the best man and couldn't have been happier. The villagers were confused by Malachi's smiles. They were a rare sight. The bridesmaid was an old school friend of Helens.

At the reception the men drank Guinness. Most of the women drank Guinness. Helen sipped at her orange juice. The band played and people danced well into the night.

Albert often thought about how fate had eventually been kind to him beyond his wildest dreams. He had been lucky to survive being killed on numerous occasions. He had seen, or been party to, the deaths of many good friends. His biggest debt though, was to the priest who gave him shelter and had enabled him to meet this woman who he hoped he would spend the rest of his life with.

Helen's return to her native country had been one of sadness after the death of her mother. She had struggled to keep the smallholding going and her days were spent worrying about the livestock and farm.

Then, suddenly her life changed when she attended the event to celebrate the life of Father Michael Creaney. She had seen Albert at the edge of the crowd. She was too shy to approach him but secretly hoped that he would come over to her.

When Aidan Doyle had finished his tribute there was a mad rush to get to the village hall. She lost sight of Albert and sadly she did not have the confidence to enter the village hall. She returned home to feed the animals.

Thank goodness Albert had made the final effort to track her down.

Albert and Helen were blissfully happy. They had used Helen's inheritance wisely. Albert had been advised by Malachi as to what farm equipment to buy and he spent the daylight hours ploughing, sewing crops and harvesting. Produce was sold to the appropriate wholesalers. He had a field of sheep which were low maintenance at the moment but he would share lambing duties with Malachi with their respective stock.

Helen had become a more accomplished cook. She was still an avid reader and always eagerly awaited the arrival of the mobile library. She shared Albert's love of classical music having been introduced by Albert to Edward Elgar and Ralph Vaughan Williams but so far had resisted his other love of Malbec red wine.

Her farm duties included catering for the hens. Three goats had a field to themselves and a braying donkey called Aidan also had his own pasture. Two Jack Russell terriers fussed round the kitchen.

Albert was relieved that Helen had not seriously questioned his past activities. Albert had told her that he had gone to Spain to find the man who had killed the priest. He told Helen that McMillan had died as the result of an accident.

He didn't tell her that McMillan had accidentally got in the way of a bullet fired from Albert's handgun.

He told her about the three friends who had helped him in Spain. When asked what had happened to them he told her that they had remained in Spain.

'Will you miss Thomas?' asked Helen.

'Yes, very much.'

71.

The morning dawned grey and cloudy with the threat of rain. Albert helped Helen clear the breakfast dishes away. As Helen was drying the plates she suddenly stopped and gasped. Through the kitchen window she had spotted a vehicle on the brow of the hill.

'Albert, look!'

Albert went to the front door of the house. At the top of his gravel drive he saw a Garda Police vehicle. As he watched he saw two uniformed officers exit from the car. They were accompanied by another figure. Albert's heart sank. The other figure was wearing a light rain coat and a dark brown trilby hat.

Detective Sergeant Ted Fuller. Albert's thought processes went into overdrive. Was Fuller here to arrest him? Or to carry out Aidan Doyle's bidding in some other form?

The three figures started to walk down the path. Albert returned to the kitchen. He put his arms round Helen.

'I don't know what this means Helen, but I just want you to know that I love you more than you can imagine and I want to be part of your life for as long as you want me.'

'Albert, I'm so frightened. Just when we'd both turned

our lives round it could all be taken away from us.'

She kissed Albert passionately on the lips.

Albert went to the front door to meet Fuller.

'I'm sorry, Albert,' said Fuller

Albert's shoulders slumped.

'I want to apologise for my sudden arrival without warning you, but I had no means of contacting you. Mister Doyle supplied your address and updated me on your personal circumstances. I felt I owed you a visit to personally inform you of the current situation.'

'Am I in trouble Sergeant Fuller?'

'Let's have a little stroll.' replied Ted Fuller. Albert grabbed his waterproof jacket. Helen looked anxiously at her husband as he left the house to join Fuller.

As they walked slowly to the field where Aidan the donkey was still braying, Detective Sergeant Fuller said,

'The Spanish police have completed their enquiries.'

Albert waited for the punch-line,

'They have no evidence against you in the case of the murder of Dennis McMillan. Circumstantial evidence is not enough on its own. Whoever shot him did a good job of covering their tracks.

'In the case of multiple murders involving the crime boss and his gang, the culprits are now deceased and they're satisfied that you were not involved in those murders. You remain a person of interest because of your close association with Henry Spearing, Thomas Cannon and Brendan Coleman. They're not seeking your arrest or extradition.

'That's a relief Sergeant Fuller, Does that mean I'm in the clear?'

'Aidan Doyle is satisfied that you don't pose a threat to his business or reputation and I hear that he was involved in your recent nuptials. Congratulations by the way. I hear that Duane was your best man.'

'Duane?'

'Duane Malachi. His parents were big fans of some old American rockstar called Duane Eddy. That's how he got cursed with that name. Since he was ten years old he was known only as Malachi.'

Albert smiled.

'Your wife is a very elegant lady and can I dare suggest that you're punching above your weight.

'I know that, Sergeant Fuller. I'm a very lucky man,' said Albert.

'There is one other matter that you should know about, Albert.'

Albert's shoulders slumped again.

'McMillan's contact in London was Detective Sergeant Elaine Webster. She was very friendly with William Cronk who attempted to kill you in Spain. She and McMillan were determined to make you pay for his death. I've evidence that she was involved in plotting your death at McMillan's hands. She is now aware that I have that evidence. Nobody wants her prosecution to go before the courts. That includes Aidan Doyle, you, Elaine Webster especially, and myself. I've had a serious chat with her, if you get my drift, and she has decided to take early retirement. She is on the point of emigrating to Canada where she will live with her sister in Vancouver.'

'I'm pleased to hear that Sergeant Fuller.'

'No problem Albert and by the way you can call me Ted. Just one other thing.'

Albert waited for the crunch statement.

'Don't you think it's time you bought me a pint of Guinness?

'That'll be my absolute pleasure, Ted.'

ACKNOWLEDGEMENTS

To everyone at The Conrad Press for giving me the opportunity to have my words published.

Rachael and Nat Ravenlock for their expertise in the presentation of this book.

My sister, Lilian Boyd for her editing skills.

My son Robert, for research and advice.

And finally, to my family for their constant support and encouragement.

Fightback is author Thomas Chaplin's debut novel. It is a fast-moving, thrilling story about people fighting back against criminality in their East London neighbourhood. The mould-breaking plot takes readers into exciting and uncharted waters.

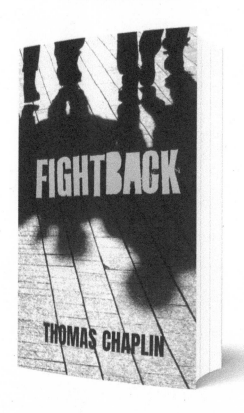

Available as a paperback and ebook.

Paperback ISBN: 978-1-914913-80-8
Ebook ISBN: 978-1-839784-90-3